KT-223-251

BOOK OF THE STARS

PART I

Quadehar
the Sorcerer

From the Chicken House

THE BOOK OF THE STARS - well, it sounded so exciting before I read a word. Children in France have been wild about it. So I asked nine-year-old Marie - the bilingual daughter of my old friend Anne who lives near Marseilles - to test it out with her friends.

They *loved* this wonderful story, of a gang of friends caught in a wild and desperately exciting fantasy, and I know you will enjoy it too.

Short chapters, funny dialogue, big magic, and a touch of romance - what more could any young reader wish for? Oh, by the way, Erik L'Homme is the author's real name - before you ask ...

Barry Cunningham
Publisher

Quadehar
the Sorcerer

Erik L'Homme
Translated by Ros Schwartz

2 Palmer Street, Frome, Somerset BA11 1DS

For Jean-Phillipe, my Master Sorcerer.
And my friends still living on The Lost Isle. ...

The publishers would like to thank
Marie Liens and Chloe Schwartz for their help with this book.

First published in France in 2001
by Gallimard Jeunesse

This edition first published in 2003 in Great Britain
by The Chicken House
2 Palmer Street
Frome, Somerset BA11 1DF
United Kingdom
www.doublecluck.com

Text © Erik L'Homme 2001
English translation © Ros Schwartz 2003
Illustrations© David Wyatt 2003

All rights reserved.
No part of this publication may be reproduced or transmitted or utilized in
any form or by any means, electronic, mechanical, photocopying or
otherwise, without the prior permission of the publisher.

Cover design by Ian Butterworth
Cover illustration by David Wyatt
Designed and typeset by Dorchester Typesetting Group Ltd
Printed and bound in Great Britain

1 3 5 7 9 10 8 6 4 2

British Library Cataloguing in Publication data available.

ISBN 1 –904442-00-5

Contents

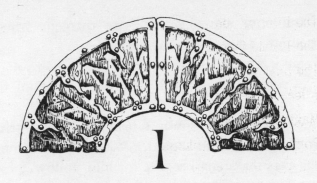

1

School's out!

The bell signalling the end of the school day was still ringing as Robin pushed through the crowds of pupils thronging towards the exit. It was early April, but the weather was already hot, and everyone was keen to go to the beach and relax, to swim if the water was warm enough, and generally let off steam after a long day of lessons.

Robin was in a hurry for a different reason – he had to be one of the first out in order to shake off Agatha Balangru and her gang and lose them in the streets of Dashtikazar.

'Come on, hurry up, you're in my way,' he muttered, barging through the boisterous crowd of students.

Behind him he heard someone yell, 'There he is, by the door!'

There was no need to turn around; he recognized the voice of Thomas Kandarisar, Agatha's sidekick. That spurred him on all the more. He reached the exit at last

7

and was now elbowing his way through when he bumped into a big third-year kid.

'Watch it, squirt!'

'Er ... sorry,' stammered Robin. 'I'm just trying to get out.'

The older boy held him in a firm grip. Panic-stricken, Robin glanced over his shoulder. With a look of triumph, Agatha was making a bee-line for him, followed by her cronies. She was tall and slim with short, dark hair, a disproportionately large mouth and a spiteful glint in her eyes.

'Drop it Marco. We'll sort him out,' hissed Agatha.

Marco hesitated, then let Robin go and ambled away with a shrug. Agatha's gang were second-years like Robin, but they were bullies, feared by the whole school, even the bigger kids.

Agatha stood facing the fugitive. Robin stared at her defiantly, his face crimson under his mop of chestnut hair.

'Little diddums looks angry,' she jeered, provoking laughter from her pals clustered around the door.

'Leave me alone! I'll never give you my pendant,' protested Robin, clenching his fists.

'We'll see about that,' retorted Agatha icily, beckoning to a stocky member of the gang, a boy with red hair.

He pounced on Robin and, after a short struggle, pinned him in an arm lock.

'Let me go, Thomas, or you'll be sorry,' threatened Robin through clenched teeth, but the boy merely sniggered.

Every inch the cruel queen, Agatha sidled over, fumbled inside her victim's collar and found the little gold sun that hung from a fine gold chain.

She yanked it off and fastened it around her own neck.

'You have no right,' he protested, still in the grip of the redhead. 'That was given to me by my father.'

'Your father? I thought you didn't know who your father was. Besides,' she sneered, bringing her face close to his, 'they say he became a Renouncer because of you!'

Robin was close to tears, but his pride stopped him and instead he stared intently at the floor. At that moment, the headmaster, a plump, middle-aged man, appeared in the corridor. His office was nearby, and the clamour of raised voices, unusual at that hour, had aroused his suspicions.

'Now you lot, what's going on?' he grumbled, annoyed at the disturbance.

'Nothing, Sir,' replied Agatha flashing him a broad smile as Thomas hastily released his grip. 'Robin was just telling us a really exciting story, wasn't he?'

The others agreed noisily. The head turned to Robin.

'A story, my boy, a story ...' he said absent-mindedly. 'Well this isn't the time or the place,' he snapped. 'Be off with you, all of you, go home! I don't want to see anyone before tomorrow morning. No, not you, Robin. You stay behind.'

Agatha's gang dispersed, darting menacing looks at Robin as they left.

'Is something the matter, son? Is there anything you want to tell me?'

9

'No, nothing at all, Sir. Honestly. May I please go now, Sir?'

The head gazed for a moment at Robin, who was trembling slightly but then he gave a shrug. 'Yes, go on then, off with you.'

Robin fled into the street and didn't stop running until he had reached the hills that overlooked the town. He flung his bag down beside a menhir, a standing stone, that had been split open by lightning and sat down on the ground. As he gazed at the ocean sparkling below, he couldn't hold back the tears any longer.

Robin had turned twelve at the Autumn equinox. He was a strong, determined boy, despite his puny appearance. But he wasn't very tall for his age, and that bothered him. How he wished he could stand up to the school bullies. His problems with Agatha and her lot had started at the beginning of term. Not because he was top of the class – he made sure his marks hovered around average, as dim-witted bullies tend to pick on the clever kids – but because he had foolishly gone to the rescue of a little first-year who was being terrorized by Agatha's gang. Since then, they'd turned their efforts to tormenting him. Somehow Robin had a habit of getting into hot water. Although he was shy, he was always rushing in and hurling himself into other people's problems. Would he ever learn to mind his own business?

Robin pushed back the stray lock of hair falling onto his forehead. His permanently tousled mop framed a delicate face that gave him a wistful expression unless broken by one of the easy smiles that made his green eyes twinkle.

Right now, Robin didn't feel like smiling at all.

He picked up a pebble and flung it angrily onto the road.

His father had decided to leave The Lost Isle to go and live in The Real World shortly before Robin was born, thus becoming a Renouncer and condemning his son to never knowing his own father. And now Agatha had stolen the precious pendant that was the only memento Robin had of him.

'I hope the Korrigans kidnap her and make her dance till her feet drop off!' cursed Robin.

He took a deep breath, relishing the salty tang of the breeze coming off the sea, and tried to forget his problems. He was a fighter by nature, and he had no intention of ever giving Agatha the satisfaction of seeing that she had upset him.

His gaze roamed over the narrow, winding streets of Dashtikazar. Huddled together, the houses with their light-grey slate roofs stood four or five storeys high. The pale granite city had celebrated its millennium the previous year. Dashtikazar the Proud ... How he loved this city so full of surprises, nestling against the mountain and looking out over the sea. It was the capital, the beating heart of the noble Lost Isle.

Robin knew from his history and geography lessons that, eight centuries ago, The Lost Isle had been a tiny section of the mainland that had broken away during a terrible storm. It had floated far out to sea, but then winds blowing inshore had driven it back again. However, The Lost Isle was now truly a lost island, caught somewhere between The Real World, which it had been a part of before, and the strange and fantastic Uncertain World. It didn't feature on any maps, and its existence had been forgotten. There was a door leading to The Real World, and another to The Uncertain World. Both doors were one-way: this precaution was The Lost Isle's only means of protection from the other two worlds. However, from time to time, when the Provost's Council felt that The Lost Isle was lacking in essential commodities such as chocolate spread or recent cinema releases, there always seemed to be a secret way of leaving and getting back again.

Little was known about The Uncertain World, other than that it was vast and full of untold danger. The Real World was very different. On The Lost Isle, it was possible to receive some radio and TV channels from the mainland, and the school curriculum was very similar to that of The Real World. Also, a select few government officials were aware of The Lost Isle's existence. These officials would help any citizens of The Lost Isle who wanted to leave the island to obtain the documents and necessary assistance to settle in Europe or elsewhere. Such people were known as Renouncers. This meant they had renounced The Lost Isle for ever. A very tiny number of them chose to venture into The Uncertain World. They were mainly those condemned to wander – the maximum sentence that could be imposed by the courts on The Lost Isle – or people seeking their fortune, adventurers and the truly desperate. These people were known as Wanderers.

As for the people who remained on The Lost Isle, their home was a large, mountainous island with dense forests and vast heaths, and scattered little towns, villages and hamlets, where it was hot in summer and cold in winter. In other words, it bore a close resemblance to The Real World, but there were some important differences.

The sound of hooves broke into Robin's thoughts. On the path, a few feet away, stood a man clad in splendid turquoise armour. There was a sword hanging at his left side and he wielded a lance that was twice the length of his horse. This grey steed wore a coat of fine steel mail that jangled with every movement.

Robin leaped to his feet.

'Is all well, my boy?' asked the knight gently.

'Yes, my lord, all is well, thank you,' he replied.

'Don't linger too long in these hills,' continued the knight, stroking his horse's neck. The animal was pawing the ground impatiently. 'It's the Korrigans' big festival at present, and you know how they love playing tricks on humans.'

With a roar of laughter, the knight bade Robin goodbye and galloped off in the direction of the town. The boy was touched. It was his secret wish, his wildest and most cherished dream, to be admitted to the Brotherhood of the Knights of the Wind one day. These knights, under the orders of their commander and the supervision of the Provost of Dashtikazar, were responsible for the security of The Lost Isle. Governed by their conscience alone, they came to the aid of all those in need.

Taking the knight's advice, Robin set off home. He lived with his mother on the edge of the village of Penmarch, a few leagues from the capital. Even if the Korrigans weren't the most dangerous creatures on The Lost Isle, they were unpredictable and their games could sometimes be cruel.

2

A wonderful surprise

'Mum! It's me! I'm home!'

Robin made straight for the kitchen and opened the fridge. He took out some butter which he put on the table next to the chocolate spread and cut a thick slice of bread from the loaf sitting on the dresser.

He was famished after his eventful day and the long trek home.

'Hello, darling? Where are you?'

'Here, inakisshen!' spluttered Robin, his mouth full.

His mother bustled into the room, smiling, and wearing a black dress, as usual. As far back as Robin could remember, his mother had always worn black. She was tall with long, wavy golden hair and azure eyes. Alicia was well and truly a Penmarch! Robin was more like his father, or at least he assumed he was, for he had not been able to glean much about him.

'How has your day been?' asked Alicia planting a kiss on her son's forehead.

'No worse than usual,' replied Robin evasively, grabbing the TV guide from a chair. 'Oh great! There's a film on tonight!'

Robin's face lit up in a big grin. His mother merely looked at him with an amused expression, her arms folded. 'Definitely no TV tonight, Robin.'

Robin uncoiled like a spring and jumped out of his chair. There weren't often films on TV, as the programmes compiled by the Cultural Commission of the Provostship tended to concentrate on reports and documentaries. So he was ready to launch into one of the long arguments that he sometimes had with his mother over television.

But she cut him short with a wave of her hand. 'Have you forgotten? It's your Uncle Urian's birthday party this evening. I know, I know, you're not very keen on him ... but the whole family will be there. The whole family and ... a few friends,' she hinted mysteriously.

Robin had half opened his mouth to protest, but now just stood there gaping. 'You mean ...?'

'Your cousin Romaric with be there, and your friend Godfrey, and the twins, Amber and Coral! Romaric and the girls are coming by to pick you up. They should be here soon. I'm going on ahead to help my brother greet the guests.'

Alicia watched her son affectionately as he danced on his chair in excitement, then she left the room to finish getting ready.

Robin raced up the stairs four at a time and burst into his room. A rapid glance reminded him that he hadn't tidied it for at least a week. He sighed and started to put things away. He and his friends always congregated in his room, and they wouldn't be ready to go to his uncle's until they'd spent at least some time chatting.

He closed his laptop, which was sitting on a stool, and stowed it in one of the drawers in his desk. Then he picked up the books strewn over the carpet and put them back in the bookcase, shook out the bedspread and smoothed it over his crumpled duvet.

Someone was knocking at the front door.

'Robin, it's us!'

'Come on up!' yelled Robin shoving the clothes that lay on the floor under the wardrobe.

A door banged, followed by laughter and the sound of feet clattering up the stairs. Two hugely excited girls and a boy burst into the room.

'It's so good to see you!' exclaimed Robin, greeting them.

'Uncle Urian's birthday must be an important one this year for us to get two whole days off school!' declared fair-haired, blue-eyed Romaric Penmarch. He was a tall, well-built boy, the exact opposite of his cousin.

'You're not complaining are you? How long is it since we've seen each other?' asked Coral Krakal, flashing one of her special smiles that made boys go weak at the knees. A stunning girl with chestnut hair, she was tall and willowy with sea-blue eyes.

'Since the Christmas holidays,' replied Amber, darting Robin a meaningful look that made him blush to the roots of his hair.

Amber and Coral were identical twins. But while Coral was always light and laughing, Amber was rather fierce and tough, and wore her hair short. Most boys were put off by her sharp tongue, but that didn't bother her – she even found it amusing. She particularly enjoyed teasing Robin. He always rose to the bait, and, despite himself, Robin felt himself turn crimson every time. But Amber was also plucky and a loyal friend, someone you could truly rely on.

'What about Godfrey?' asked Robin to escape Amber's mocking gaze. 'Didn't he come?'

'Of course he did!' Romaric reassured him. 'But he's gone directly up to the castle to help his parents carry their instruments. You should have seen the chaos when we left. It looked as though they were moving house!'

Romaric and Godfrey lived close to each other at the other end of The Lost Isle, in the little town of Bounic, two days away by cart from Penmarch. Amber and Coral lived nearer, on the east coast of the island, in the village of Krakal where their father, Utigern, was both mayor and Qamdar – the clan chief. Utigern was chief of the Krakal clan, just as Urian, Robin and Romaric's uncle, was chief of the Penmarch clan. That was why the Krakals had been invited to the birthday party.

As for Godfrey's parents, they were the greatest musicians on The Lost Isle and no party was complete without them.

'I wish I could have seen that,' exclaimed Robin, 'Godfrey having to carry all that gear ... I can just imagine him whinging about his hair getting messed up!'

'It'll toughen him up a bit, he's such a wimp,' smiled Amber pulling a face and glaring at her sister who was preening herself in front of one of the windows.

They all laughed.

'Dad says everybody who's anybody on The Lost Isle will be at the party,' chirped Coral as she joined the others, who were already sprawled on the thick goatskin rug.

'And not only the Penmarch clan's friends,' added Amber. 'Urian also sent invitations to enemy families. To try and ease tensions.'

'Enemy families ... like the Balangrus and the Kandarisars?' asked Robin, his face clouding over.

'Don't tell me that witch Agatha and that scum Thomas are still hassling you?' fumed Romaric. 'If I could go to your school instead of you just once! I'd soon teach them not to pick on people smaller than them!'

Romaric bit his lip, immediately wishing he could take back his words. Robin smiled glumly.

'In any case,' Romaric went on, determined to make up for his blunder, 'you won't be on your own tonight. Just let them try coming near our clan!'

The words were no sooner out of his mouth when Amber whooped and executed a war dance.

With a yell, Romaric joined in, laughing, 'Come Agatha the Witch and Thomas the Snitch, come try your strength against Romaric's muscles of steel, Godfrey the Great, Coral the Fairy Queen, Amber the Ruthless and Robin the Knight!'

Coral clapped and then, her eyes shining, announced,

'I can't wait for the ball. I love dancing too!'

'What you love is watching the poor idiots falling over themselves to ask you to dance,' chipped in Amber scornfully. 'I hope there'll be knights there ... real ones.'

'And I'll be happy just to eat,' said Romaric. 'Uncle always has amazing food! What about you, Robin?'

'Me,' sighed Robin, who couldn't help thinking about his stolen pendant. He wasn't particularly looking forward to going to his uncle's. 'I'd rather stay here, just us, out of the way of Agatha and her gang.'

'So do something about it! This is Penmarch territory; *she's* the one who should be feeling scared!' retorted Amber, shaking him gently by the shoulder. 'And stop thinking about that horrid girl for a minute, will you? There are other girls, you know.'

She shot him another look that made him blush scarlet again and the others all burst out laughing.

'It's nearly time to leave,' announced Romaric checking his watch. 'If I turn up late, I'll be in big trouble.'

'Oh, poor baby!' simpered Coral.

'His daddy'll be cross with him!' taunted Amber pummelling him playfully.

'Stop it, you lot, it's not funny,' protested Romaric hurling a cushion at the nearest assailant.

3

A well-deserved slap

Urian Penmarch's mansion stood on a hill outside the village. It was a two-storey building protected by thick stone walls and flanked by square towers, as was customary in the region. It was more like a medieval castle than a country retreat, for it was not so long since the days when there were frequent quarrels between the main clans of The Lost Isle.

'Hurry up!' panted Romaric at the head of the little group hurrying towards the Penmarch stronghold.

'Slow down, Romaric,' puffed Robin. 'Look, we're not the last.'

The four crossed the paved courtyard where horse-drawn carriages were dropping off the guests dressed in party clothes. There were no motor vehicles on The Lost Isle as anything that caused heavy pollution was banned. Electricity came from the huge windmills on the Turbulent Moors, and from discreetly positioned solar panels for domestic use. Homes were heated by wood fires, or by means of an ingenious system for capturing natural ground heat.

'Where did you get to?' complained the white-haired man greeting the guests at the door. 'Lord Penmarch has been asking after you.'

'Good evening, Valentino!' said Amber with a smile. 'Sorry, we were dancing ... with the Korrigans!'

'Little monsters,' said the doorman.

'Good evening, Valentino.' Coral greeted him with a kiss.

'Good evening, Valentino,' chorused Romaric and Robin, shadow boxing.

'Everyone is in the great hall,' announced Valentino. 'It's nearly time for the old bore's speech!'

They laughed at his impudence. Valentino was much more than the doorman; he was also the estate manager, the butler, the steward and Urian Penmarch's right-hand man who, in times gone by, had accompanied him on all his exploits.

Shooed along by him, the friends entered the mansion and walked down a long corridor that led to a vast hall, echoing with the clamour of voices. There was a huge fire burning in the hearth.

'Oh no,' groaned Robin, 'she's already here.'

'Where?' asked Coral glancing eagerly about her.

'Near Dad, over by the buffet,' Amber informed her grimly. 'Does she think it's carnival or what?'

Agatha Balangru, her face caked in make-up, caught sight of them and gave a provocative little wave.

'Forget it, Robin,' sighed Romaric. 'Let's go and rescue

Godfrey from the clutches of our uncle instead.'

The little group headed towards a giant with a bushy grey beard, who was holding forth in a loud voice, roaring with laughter after every word. Several people were clustered around him, including a boy who looked bored out of his mind.

It was Godfrey Grum, an unusually tall boy with carefully combed black hair.

'Aha!' bellowed Urian Penmarch. 'Here's the Penmarch clan at last!'

'Accompanied by their loyal friends, Uncle,' replied Romaric caught in the embrace of the colossal man whose overwhelming presence had never intimidated him. 'Here are Amber and Coral Krakal.'

'My beauties!' exclaimed Urian, almost crushing the twins in a bear hug. 'I'd never have thought that old fox Utigern was capable of producing such pretty daughters!'

Then he turned to Godfrey whose face had lit up at the arrival of the gang, 'I'm delighted to have met you, young Grum. And I hope you're as talented as your parents,' he declared, crushing Godfrey's shoulder.

He then sent them packing with a huge guffaw, greeting Robin with a simple pat on the cheek, and resumed his conversation. The two cousins, followed by their three friends, threaded their way towards the fireplace.

'Can someone tell me if I still have a right shoulder?' Godfrey winced.

'What a man!' enthused Coral.

'Yes, I'm his spitting image,' retorted Robin

sarcastically. He never knew whether to be pleased or annoyed at his uncle's coolness towards him.

'How come it took you so long to get here?' complained Godfrey. 'I don't mind carrying my mother's harp, even if it does weigh a ton, but standing there while your uncle thumps me is torture!'

'Don't you complain,' answered Romaric. 'Some people would give their right arm to be introduced to Urian Penmarch.'

'And even to have him thump them on the back!' chipped in Robin.

Romaric gave his cousin a slightly awkward hug, glad that his banter had cheered him up again.

'A little family reunion, how touching,' sneered a voice behind them.

They spun round. Facing them stood Agatha and her loyal sidekick, Thomas Kandarisar, his hair more fiery and his frame more massive than ever.

'What a pity,' she went on, 'that a man like Urian has nobody to succeed him but a little wimp and an ugly brute.'

Romaric lunged at her with a roar, but was intercepted by Thomas. The two were matched in strength, so the fight was short lived, as Thomas backed away.

'Tut, tut, Romaric,' taunted Agatha shaking her head with a mocking smile. 'Hitting a girl. That's no way for a would-be knight to behave!'

'I'm a girl too,' piped up Amber. 'What do have to say to this?'

Before anyone had the chance to say a word, Amber

had shot forward and slapped the taller girl, who froze in astonishment. Urian Penmarch chose that moment to call for attention and demand silence.

'You'll pay for that!' seethed Agatha, pointing at Amber who stood with her arms folded and a smug grin. 'As for the rest of you ...'

She didn't finish her sentence. She turned abruptly on her heel and, followed by a dejected Thomas, rejoined her family circle by the buffet.

'Hey, sis, you have no dress sense, but when it comes to slapping, you're the best!' whispered Coral proudly.

'I wonder whether we should write a poem in commemoration of this great deed,' murmured Godfrey mischievously in Romaric's ear, while Amber quietly savoured her triumph.

'Thank you,' was all Robin could muster.

'In any case, there's no chance of being bored with you lot around. It's good to see you,' said Godfrey, overjoyed at being reunited with his friends.

After Urian Penmarch had thanked his guests for coming, lectured on the need for everyone to live peacefully with their neighbours and received the customary congratulations on his youthful looks on the eve of his sixtieth birthday, everyone was invited to eat, drink and be merry. The village musicians launched into a lively piece, and a buzz of conversation and merriment filled the room once more.

Robin and his gang were at the buffet. Scanning the room for his mother, he had caught sight of his giant of an uncle talking with a man he hadn't seen before. And this man fascinated him. First of all, he wore the long dark cloak of the Wizards and Sorcerers of the Guild, the ancient institution that was responsible for the safety of The Lost Isle on the magic front, in the same way that the Brotherhood of Knights operated on the practical level. It was rare to meet a sorcerer outside of the monasteries, where they lived a reclusive existence. But there was something else that mesmerized Robin: this man seemed to be watching him ...

'Hey, Robin, wake up,' said Romaric tugging his sleeve. 'There won't be any food left! Here, have a bite of this doughnut! And just taste this honey beer, it's delicious!'

Robin tore his eyes away from the stranger and tried his best to do justice to the banquet. How he wished he were like his cousin! Everything seemed much easier when he was around. There was no doubt that one day Romaric would be admitted to the Brotherhood of Knights, something they had both dreamed of since they were tiny. Whereas he, Robin ... Although he was scrawny, he knew he wasn't weak, but he wasn't exceptionally strong either. And the same was true of everything else. He was good at school but not brilliant, a good musician but not talented, a good friend but not always much fun. He sometimes wondered what the others saw in him, how they could enjoy his company. It was hardly surprising really that Romaric has always been Urian's favourite. Even though his mother told him he was mistaken, he knew he had never been welcome at the Penmarches. He suddenly felt like a dwarf in comparison. Perhaps, when he came of age, he should follow in his father's footsteps and become a Renouncer, even though his mother would be heartbroken. Maybe that was the only way he'd ever find his place in the world.

Suddenly there was a commotion as several men came and pushed the tables back against the walls, while others brought huge jugs of beer and wine. Valentino clambered onto a chair and cupping his hands announced: 'Ladies and gentlemen, the ball!'

Romaric sighed, while Coral looked ready to burst with excitement.

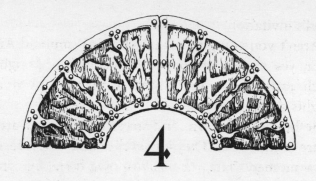

4

An eventful end to the party

As Amber had predicted, a dozen or so teenage boys, the sons of the foremost families in the land, were eagerly pursuing Coral, who amused herself by ranking them according to their talents on the dance floor.

She was soon being whirled across the great hall by a boy who was vain as a peacock. A dozen or so other couples were moving effortlessly to the music.

'I hate dancing,' said Romaric to his friends who were watching with interest.

'You only say that because you refuse to learn,' retorted Godfrey. 'I like dancing. The only problem is I always end up with the clumsy girls!'

Right on cue, a girl came up, stepped on his toe and asked him to dance. Godfrey followed her, putting his hands around his neck in a strangling gesture. It was considered rude for a boy who could dance to turn down a girl's invitation.

'Aren't you going to ask me, Robin?' smirked Amber.

'Er, yes ... yes, of course,' he replied, although he'd much rather have sat talking with his cousin about knights and chivalry.

He held out his arm and steered Amber towards the centre of the room. They joined the circle of dancers, and a few moments later, he was skipping beside his partner.

'Huh!' snorted Romaric to himself, turning to the table and pouring himself a big mug of corma, the traditional honey brew of The Lost Isle.

He may not be able to dance, but you didn't need to dance to be a knight! You just had to be hardy, brave and a skilled swordsman. He shrugged and chided himself. OK, he had to admit that he didn't enjoy it, his parents didn't dance in front of him every evening, like Godfrey's, and his mother had never made him have lessons, like Robin's. And yet. ... Maybe he wouldn't find parties so boring if he made the effort to learn? If only he dared. Especially as the dances of The Lost Isle didn't look anything like those of The Real World, which they showed on TV. Here, people danced in a group, there was always someone to show you the steps and nobody laughed at your mistakes. You laughed and had fun, and everyone always had a good time.

Romaric finished his drink and made a decision ... *there was no time like the present.*

Valentino climbed onto his chair again and called for the guests' attention.

'Ladies and gentlemen, a musical interlude!'

Fanning themselves, the dancers left the floor for a drink, while Godfrey's parents set up their instruments on the podium – a little organ and a big harp. Then they began to play. Their music was hauntingly beautiful, and everyone sat spellbound long after the last note had died away. The Grums' performance was greeted with thunderous clapping and shouts of *encore!*

Smiling, Godfrey's mother rose and addressed the audience. 'Thank you so much for your generous applause. Sadly, as you all know, custom prevents us from playing more than one piece this evening. ...'

There were protests. Mrs Grum held up a hand to pacify the crowd.

'However, there's another member of the family who you haven't heard yet. He will now play something for you. Please welcome our son Godfrey.'

Robin nudged Godfrey, who was stunned by his mother's announcement. He had never been asked to play formally in public before.

'Go on, Godfrey,' whispered his friend. 'This is your chance to show them what you can do!'

'Supposing I mess up?' protested Godfrey, reluctant to go and join his parents, who were encouraging him to go up on stage.

'You can do it!' urged Romaric. 'There are opportunities that have to be grasped, and I think this is one of them!'

'Thanks for the pressure,' moaned Godfrey as he stumbled towards the musicians to the applause of the guests.

His mother smiled at him as he climbed up onto the stage, and his father handed him a zither, a guitar-like instrument played flat, which Godfrey liked to practise on.

'Thanks a bunch!' he said between clenched teeth.

'We know you can do it, darling,' replied his mother.

'Besides,' added his father sternly, 'the time has come for you to show what you can do.'

Godfrey took a deep breath. He caught sight of Robin, Amber, Coral and Romaric at the back of the room, making encouraging signs.

'Show what I can do? All right. They'll see – or rather hear!' he said to himself.

He cleared his throat. 'Ladies and gentlemen,' he announced in a clear voice, 'this evening, I'm not going to play you something from the classical repertoire, but one of my own compositions instead.'

Murmurs of astonishment rippled through the audience. It was years since a musician had been so bold as to propose something new, as the people of The Lost Isle were renowned for their resistance to change.

The air was filled with silent anticipation. Godfrey began to play. It was a delightful tune, and boldly original. His fervour made up for his lack of experience. Then he opened his mouth and began to sing. The sweetness of his voice and the simple words evoking the beauties of his native town of Bounic enthralled the audience. Even the Sorcerer of the Guild sat smiling and nodding.

Godfrey's performance was greeted with thunderous

applause, and his delighted father gave him an emotional hug.

'Bravo, Godfrey!' shouted Romaric when their friend was able to tear himself away from his mother, who was flushed with pride, and Urian Penmarch, who had come over to congratulate him.

'Pity I wasn't able to give it my all,' replied Godfrey smoothing his hair with an air of false modesty.

'Why not?' asked Coral.

'Because a bunch of idiots waving at the back of the room ruined my concentration!' he teased.

The gang pelted him with bread balls.

'Did you notice the sorcerer while Godfrey was playing?' Robin asked the others.

'No,' Romaric replied, surprised. 'What about him?'

'Er ... nothing,' was all Robin could answer. 'He seemed to be enjoying it, that's all.'

'And since when have you been interested in sorcerers?' teased Amber, seeing a chance to tease him.

'Since ... never. I'm not especially interested in sorcerers! Well, that is ...'

'Drop it,' said Romaric, coming to his rescue, and ... let's go and dance!' he added for the benefit of the others who couldn't believe their ears. 'Come on, the dance music's started again!'

'Did you hear that?' burst out Coral in amazement, 'I want to be the lucky girl!'

They made their way over to the flagstone floor where she tried to teach him the steps of a square dance.

A little later, Romaric came back alone. 'I'm not bad,

apparently,' he panted. 'But I was unlucky. That was an especially difficult dance!'

'And,' cut in Amber, 'my sister ditched you for a more talented beau!'

'Shut up!' Robin interrupted. 'Look, there's an argument over there, by the fire!'

Two men were hurling insults at each other and looked as though they were about to start fighting.

'It's Daddy!' exclaimed Amber in amazement.

'And Agatha's father!' added Godfrey, horrified.

The quarrel was growing more bitter. Urian Penmarch, assisted by Valentino and a few others, was trying in vain to separate the two men. Above the din, the host's deep voice could be heard booming: 'Gentlemen! Gentlemen!' to no avail. Without warning, the two men unsheathed their swords and confronted each other. Amber turned pale and bit her lip. At that moment, the man in the dark cloak, the Sorcerer of the Guild, stepped between them, raised his arms and uttered a few words in a strange whisper. The two swords instantly disintegrated and turned to dust.

The sorcerer then turned to the bewildered guests and addressed the gathering. 'People of The Lost Isle! You appear not to have learned anything from the evil deeds of The Shadow. The Lost Isle is a fragile country, not without enemies! It is vital for us to be united, not divided, and put our petty squabbles behind us!'

The combatants' thirst for battle had vanished along with their swords, leaving lords Krakal and Balangru looking rather shamefaced in the centre of the circle of guests that had formed around them.

'The incident is closed!' thundered Urian Penmarch. 'Let the dancing continue!'

It was a while before the party was in full swing again; everybody was excitedly discussing the intervention of the sorcerer who had dared name The Shadow without fear. The Shadow was a terrifying and mysterious creature from The Uncertain World that had made several appearances on The Lost Isle, leaving a trail of havoc and destruction. The Balangru clan had hurriedly left the room, and soon the castle. Amber and Coral had run for comfort into the arms of their father who tried to reassure everyone by dismissing the subject of the quarrel, declaring it was because they'd had too much to drink. Uncle Urian was conversing with the man from the Guild and thanking him for his help.

Suddenly Romaric shouted, 'Robin! Look at Robin!'

Robin was floating above the table, unconscious, revealing the whites of his eyes. A hush fell over the room and everyone stared in amazement. Alicia made to rush over to her son, but the sorcerer restrained her, saying authoritatively, 'Leave him, there's nothing to worry about. Trust me.'

5

A strange visitor

'Good morning, darling, how are you feeling today?' Alicia asked her son as she placed a tray containing a hearty breakfast on his bedside table.

'Not too bad,' replied Robin, sitting up in bed.

'I've brought you your favourite – bread and butter with lashings of chocolate spread!'

'Mmm! Great!'

'I don't know how you can eat that stuff,' remarked Alicia, and sat down on the bed.

'It's easy,' Robin explained, taking a big bite out of the bread. 'Look, Mum – I open my mouth, put the bread and chocolate spread inside and I chew.'

'Don't be cheeky!' replied his mother, affectionately ruffling his hair.

Then she stood up and began tidying the room. Robin wolfed down his breakfast while his mother picked up the books and computer disks scattered around the bed.

Robin hadn't left his room for three days now. When

he had been brought home unconscious from Uncle Urian's, Alicia Penmarch had been out of her mind with worry. Luckily, it was not long before Robin was back to his old self and soon he felt as right as rain. But his mother had insisted he stay in bed for a while, and the doctor had even given him a letter that exempted him from school. Robin hadn't protested. Three days off school was always a treat!

His mother came over and placed her hand on his forehead to see if he had a temperature.

'The doctor said you can go back to school tomorrow,' she announced, pleased.

'Oh great,' cried Robin pulling a face.

Just then, there was a knock on the front door.

'See you later,' said Alicia. 'Don't spend too long playing on the computer. Try and rest, darling.'

She hurried downstairs. Robin sighed. He should have put his forehead against the radiator when his mother wasn't looking. Then he could have avoided lessons (and Agatha!) for the rest of the week. But that wasn't a solution and he knew it. He mentally ran through the classes he'd missed. Today was maths and fencing. He'd catch up at the weekend. Yesterday and the day before, though, were more of a problem. Swimming (he'd try to go swimming tomorrow so he wouldn't be behind), Korrigani (the Korrigans' language, which he hated), physics and chemistry (at the moment they were learning the very complicated wind chart of The Lost Isle) and Ska (the language spoken in The Uncertain World, which they were taught as part of their general education. That was easy). He let out another sigh – he wasn't going to have much time to himself after school *this* week.

The sound of the stairs creaking broke into his thoughts.

'Mum! Who was it at the door?'

There was no reply. The footsteps stopped outside his door.

'Mum? Is that you?'

Robin's heart began to race. Something weird was happening. He strained to listen. There were no other sounds from downstairs. The stairs began to creak again.

'Mum?'

No reply. This was beginning to feel scary. Robin leaped out of bed in his sky-blue pyjamas. He didn't stop to get dressed, but scrambled over to the cupboard. He pulled out the foil he used for fencing practice at school, and tiptoed back to wait behind the door. The handle slowly began to turn – *somebody was coming in.* Somebody who was planning to take him by surprise, and who had perhaps already hurt his mother down-stairs! The very thought made Robin tighten his grip on his weapon.

A dark shape slid noiselessly into the room. Robin just caught a glimpse of a tall man dressed in a voluminous cloak. He brandished his sword and fell upon the intruder with a shout. In a split second, the man span round, blocking Robin's arm, and took away his foil.

'Whoa, my boy. That's a funny way of welcoming a visitor!'

Still stunned from having been overpowered so

quickly, Robin didn't immediately recognize his adversary.

'You're the sorcerer! The sorcerer who was at the party!' he almost shouted.

He could hardly believe his eyes.

'That's right, my boy,' confirmed his visitor, gazing at him benevolently.

He was a tallish, well-built man with very short hair and a square jaw. His steel-blue eyes gave him a hard look that was at odds with his soft voice and gentle smile. It was hard to tell his age, but he probably wasn't as old as he seemed. Under the dark cloak of the Guild, he wore sturdy, comfortable clothes like any other traveller, and he carried a canvas shoulder bag.

He made Robin sit down on the edge of the bed, and then sat down beside him.

'You're not lacking in courage, son. But you were much too slow off the mark!'

'What have you done with my mother?' Robin broke in angrily. He didn't like the way this man was making fun of him.

'Your mother? I think she's making me a cup of tea, in the kitchen. ...'

'You're lying!' accused Robin who could feel tears welling up in his eyes.

'Come, my boy, calm down! It's true, I should have knocked first, I'm sorry I gave you a scare. But I assure you, your mother's fine!'

Just then, there was the sound of lighter footsteps on the stairs and, a few moments later, Alicia Penmarch came into the room carrying a tray with a cup and a steaming pot of tea. Robin shot her a questioning look. 'Are you OK, Mum?'

'Of course I'm OK, darling. Why?'

Robin suddenly felt very stupid.

'No, nothing ...'

'I'll leave you to it,' chirped Alicia putting the tray down on the bed. 'Master Quadehar, I'll be in the kitchen if you need me.' She left, closing the door behind her.

Robin realized he'd been mistaken, the sorcerer was simply a visitor, whom his mother seemed to know, and whose only offence was to have given him a shock! He switched his concentration to the reason for this visit. What did this strange man want of him, and why was his mother so keen to leave the two of them alone? He curbed his curiosity and waited for the sorcerer to finish his tea.

Smacking his lips with satisfaction, the man put the cup back on the tray and turned to Robin. 'Now, tell me about this fainting of yours?'

There was something in the sorcerer's voice that made Robin suddenly feel he could trust him after all.

'Oh, it's finished, now. The doctor says I'm better and can go back to school tomorrow.'

The man chuckled. His warm laugh put Robin completely at ease.

'My name is Quadehar. Master Quadehar. As for your doctor, he's a fool!'

Robin was at a loss for words.

The sorcerer went on, 'He's a fool, because you weren't ill in the first place. Have you ever heard of the Tarquin effect?'

Robin shook his head.

'What class are you in, my boy?'

'I'm in the second year of high school, Sir ... I mean Master Quadehar.'

'Of course. ... It's quite natural,' went on the sorcerer. 'You don't start studying the history of the Guild and the Brotherhood until next year. ... Well, Tarquin was a boy who lived on The Lost Isle three hundred years ago. He was a totally ordinary boy. Then, one day, when he was watching a sorcerers' duel – they were always fighting duels in those days – he fainted and rose off the ground. Just like you!'

'Then what?' urged Robin impatiently.

'Tarquin came round after two days and the incident was forgotten. Later, he entered the Guild as an apprentice and showed an extraordinary talent for magic. He was so gifted that he became the youngest ever Grand Master of the Guild, and developed new fields of magic. Some learned members of the Guild made the connection between his youthful fainting fit and his talents as a sorcerer. Since then, the reaction that some children have to magic has been known as "the Tarquin effect".'

There was a silence. Robin's head was spinning. Quadehar just watched him, smiling contentedly.

'And ... er, did I act like Tarquin? I mean,' stammered the boy, 'did I have a reaction to the magic?'

'Yes, my boy,' confirmed the sorcerer. 'It was when I

invoked the magic powers to turn the swords to dust that
you fainted and rose up into the air.'

'And ... what will happen now?' asked Robin
anxiously.

The man reassured him. 'Nothing at all! You're not
ill. And you can carry on with your life as before.
However ...'

The sorcerer stared hard at him.

'However, Master Quadehar?' repeated Robin
nervously.

'Don't worry, my boy,' continued Quadehar. 'everything's fine! I was just thinking that like Tarquin and
others before you, you probably have a talent for magic.
And, as I plan to stay in the area for a while, I wondered
whether you might agree to become my apprentice.'

Robin was speechless. First his fainting, then this man
was inviting to become a sorcerer, no less. It was all a bit
much to take in at once. Why couldn't he just be left
alone? Hadn't he enough problems as it was? When it
wasn't Agatha's gang, it was a so-called Tarquin effect!
What next? And then above all, above all ...

Robin felt overwhelmed. He knew that some children,
around the age of thirteen, became sorcerers' apprentices. But he had never wondered how, for the simple
reason that he wanted to be a knight, not a sorcerer! So,
one day, he hoped to be a squire. The problem was that
a squire couldn't become a sorcerer, and nor could an
apprentice become a knight.

Intrigued by his silence, Quadehar asked him, 'Is
something the matter? If you're worrying about your

mother or your uncle, I have no doubt I can get them to agree! If you're concerned about your school work, don't worry, we'll only work together some evenings, when you're off school, and on Sundays.'

'No,' Robin tried to explain. There was a lump in his throat. 'It's ... it's the Brotherhood. It's always been my dream to become a Knight of the Wind!'

Quadehar's expression became serious. 'I understand. So consider carefully, and think long and hard before you make up your mind. For, as you no doubt know, even though sorcerers and knights work together, if you agree to follow my teaching, you will never be able to enter the Brotherhood.'

Robin was at a loss. What should he do? If he agreed, he would forfeit all his chances of ever wearing the turquoise armour of the knights whose exploits had fascinated him for as long as he'd been old enough to listen to stories! And the world of the Guild and the sorcerers had always seemed weird ... frightening even. What would he find? What magic were these men hiding in the folds of their cloaks? He'd never find out if he said no. Something Romaric had said suddenly came into his mind. His cousin had said to Godfrey, just before his triumph: *There are opportunities that have to be grasped, and I think this is one of them!*

Maybe this was his big opportunity now. He decided to trust his instincts, and, gazing deep into the sorcerer's cold eyes, he asked him, 'Do you really think I should say yes?'

'Yes, Robin, I do,' replied Quadehar without hesitation.

The boy looked pensive, then nodded with conviction.

'OK, I accept,' he blurted out, taking the plunge. 'But you'll have to persuade my mother and my uncle!'

Quadehar gave a smile of satisfaction and rose from the bed where he had been sitting all the while. 'I'll deal with it. But first of all, we must have a formal agreement.'

He rummaged in his bag and took out a piece of charcoal. 'This charcoal is from the wood of a yew tree, the most magic tree of all.'

He went over to Robin, took his right hand and drew on his palm with the charcoal. 'That is the sign of obedience, which is essential for every student.'

He also drew something on the palm of his own hand. 'The sign of patience, essential for every teacher. Now, repeat after me: "I, Robin, agree to study magic and take Quadehar as my master".'

Robin repeated the words, sensing the weight of the promise.

Then it was Quadehar's turn to declare: 'I, Quadehar, Sorcerer of the Guild, agree to teach magic and take Robin as my apprentice.'

Then they shook hands firmly, smudging the charcoal lines.

'You won't regret it, Robin. Trust me. ...'

Robin hoped he was right, with all his heart, because it was too late to change his mind now.

6

Alicia Penmarch

Ensconced in his armchair of solid Tantreval oak, where he liked to sit and think as evening fell, Urian Penmarch gazed at the flames dancing in the fireplace. The only sound in the vast, silent room was the crackling of the chestnut logs.

Beside him, sitting on a stool, Valentino stretched his long legs and held his palms towards the fire to warm his hands. A log rolled into the hearth, and the butler picked it up with the heavy tongs and put it back on the fire.

'Damn the pair of them!' groaned Urian. 'How dare they do that to me! Utigern and that fool Balangru ruined my birthday party!'

'Come now, Urian,' Valentino tried to soothe him, 'let bygones be bygones. After all, nobody got hurt.'

'Nobody got hurt?' roared the giant, gripping the arms of his huge chair. 'If Quadehar hadn't been there, those two idiots could have run their swords through each other!'

'Talking of Quadehar,' Valentino hastily replied, trying to change the subject, 'isn't Alicia coming here this evening to talk about him?'

Urian looked peeved and leaned back in his chair.

Surprised at receiving no reply to his question, Valentino went on, 'What's going on? Is something the matter?'

Suddenly, it dawned on him that Urian's irritability had nothing to do with the unfortunate incident at the party, but that something more serious was upsetting his master. He waited patiently for Lord Penmarch to confide in him.

'Would you believe,' Urian announced gloomily, 'that Quadehar has requested Robin as his apprentice?'

Valentino was flabbergasted. His face was the picture of astonishment. 'But, but ... it isn't possible!'

Urian suddenly rose and began to pace up and down in front of the fireplace, tormented by all sorts of anxieties.

'No, of course, it isn't possible,' he said finally. 'And that's precisely what I shall tell my sister. And she'll have to listen to me. I'm head of this family after all.'

Somewhere in the vast mansion, a door banged and the sound of footsteps echoed in the corridors.

'That must be her,' said Valentino. 'Shall I leave?'

'Do as you like,' grumbled Urian. 'You and I have no secrets from each other, do we, my old companion?'

The two men exchanged a profound look of understanding.

Then they turned to the door as Alicia came into the room.

As usual, Alicia Penmarch was dressed in black; the midnight tone emphasized the paleness of her bare forearms and the clear blue of her large eyes.

She had just turned thirty-one and was a woman of great beauty. But there was an immense sadness in her face.

She went over to the fire. 'Mmm, it's nice and warm in here. There was a horrid icy wind blowing all the way to the castle. How are you, Urian? Valentino?'

'Very well, thank you,' replied the butler. 'May I offer you a cup of tea, to warm you up? Or some hot chocolate?'

'Tea will be lovely, thank you, Valentino!' said the young woman with a smile. 'And what about you, brother dear, you haven't answered me,' she went on as the butler left the room and headed for the kitchens.

'I'm fine, I'm fine,' grunted the giant, scratching his beard.

'You don't look it,' replied Alicia staring at him.

'No, as a matter of fact, I'm not fine!' exploded Urian Penmarch. 'What's all this ridiculous business about Robin and sorcery?'

Alicia was lost for words for a moment. Then she spoke, struggling to remain calm. 'This ridiculous business, as you call it, may turn out to be a very good thing. Master Quadehar, Sorcerer of the Guild ...'

'I know Quadehar!' broke in Urian. 'He's a fine man, I've nothing against him.'

'So what's the problem?' asked Alicia raising her voice too. 'Well? You're the one who's always telling all and sundry that my son is a good-for-nothing! That he's a misfit on The Lost Isle! And now a sorcerer turns up, announces that Robin has all the makings of a good apprentice, and you turn your nose up and say—'

'I say no!' he thundered. 'No, no, no! That boy will have nothing to do with the Guild! Do you hear me? I forbid it!'

Alicia looked her brother up and down in scorn.

'To think how I've always supported you in front of my son, whereas you've always hated him and he's always known it. ...'

She went over to Urian Penmarch whose anger had cooled at his sister's unusually frosty tone.

'Listen to me, Urian, listen carefully ...'

Her gaze was as hard as the steel of a sword.

'This is the second time in my life that you have forbidden me something. The first time, I gave in, to my regret. This time, I intend to stand up to you, for the sake of my son's happiness!'

'This is no time to drag up the past, but—' Urian tried to interrupt her.

'Be quiet, I haven't finished! This is what is going to happen: I am going to allow Robin to be apprenticed to this sorcerer, and in exchange for your consent, I'm prepared to forget the conversation we've had this evening. So that, in my heart, I can still think of you as my dear brother.'

Alicia shot Urian one last look that sent a shiver down his spine, then she turned on her heel and marched out.

'Has she gone?' asked Valentino setting down a tray

on the coffee table next to the armchair where Urian
Penmarch was sitting once more.

'Yes.'

'And?'

'And nothing. I'm getting old and weary, Valentino. I
sometimes feel more like Alicia's father than her older
brother.'

The butler smiled and placed a hand on his friend's
shoulder.

'It's true we're not as young as we were in those distant
days when we were fearless knights fighting for honour
and peace on The Lost Isle!'

'You're right, those days are long gone,' sighed Urian.
'I've always refused to think about them, as I've always
believed that taking refuge in the past is a way of running
away from the future. But what does the future hold for
us, my friend? Isn't our life behind us?'

'Don't be so melodramatic,' said Valentino soothingly.
He too was growing emotional.

They fell silent, lost in thought as they gazed into the
fire.

'She's an impressive woman, your sister,' said
Valentino after a while.

'Yes, she's a Penmarch through and through.'

'So is Robin, Urian, so is Robin. Isn't it time ...?'

Lord Penmarch's scathing look prevented him from
saying any more and he sighed. Valentino got up, put
another log on the fire and took the cold tea back to the
kitchen, leaving Urian to brood.

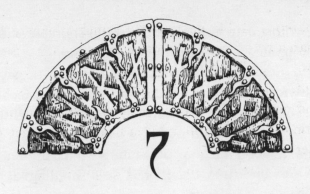

7

A great day

'I felt, yes ... I felt something ... something powerful ... something I'd been anticipating for a long time, for a very long time. ... To think that I'd been seeking the child in this world ... all those years ... when he wasn't there. ...'

'Master? Master, is everything all right?'

The young man with a shaven head and dressed in a white tunic, gingerly approached the shape in the shadows in the far corner of the room with grey stone walls.

The place was full of furniture covered with the most incredible jumble of instruments and papers.

'Yes, yes. ... Everything's fine. ... Absolutely fine. ...'

The young man stopped in his tracks. The powerful, hollow whisperings of the man he addressed as Master were beginning to make his blood run cold.

'Bring me a drink. We must celebrate. Today is a great day.'

The young man rushed up the spiral staircase without even stopping to close the door behind him.

In the gloom, the shape moved and began to pace up and down the far end of the room, which was feebly lit by the dim rays that filtered in from a skylight. He seemed to trail his shadow in his wake.

'Soon. ... Soon the hour of triumph will be upon us. ...'

The servant came back breathless, holding a large metal goblet. He stopped to wipe the beads of sweat from his forehead on the sleeve of his tunic and nervously made his way across the room. 'Your corma, Master.'

'Put it down over there. ...'

The boy obeyed and then took a step back.

The mysterious form went over to the table. What could have seemed an illusion, from a distance, was not: the darkness moved with him! And the form concealed in the shadows, though unquestionably human, was barely visible. A dark veil seemed to come down over the goblet of corma.

'I raise my glass to Tarquin ... and to all those whom the Tarquin effect has brought into the light. ...'

The Master chortled nastily. The young man in the tunic prayed to Bohor the Almighty to end his ordeal soon. He loathed this tower, he loathed this room, full of strange objects and indecipherable books! Nobody liked answering the Master's summons, and the servants would toss a coin to see who would go. He always seemed to lose.

'Go and find Lomgo for me ... and tell him to bring pen and paper. ...'

The servant didn't need to be told twice and, mentally thanking Bohor, who had answered his prayer so quickly, vanished up the staircase again.

Shortly afterwards, someone else entered the dark room. Tall and thin, his head shaven like that of the servant, he had gimlet eyes and even looked like a bird of prey. The scribe didn't seem at all afraid of the mysterious form. 'You sent for me, Master?'

'Yes. ... Sit down, Lomgo, and take note. ... Then you will go in person and deliver the missive to our friend. ... Not forgetting the gold that always goes with it. ...'

Another unpleasant chortling sound filled the room.

Lomgo gave a little smile. 'You seem in good spirits, Master.'

'Yes, I'm in excellent spirits ... I haven't been in such good spirits for an eternity.'

'Is it because of the good omen you discovered in the entrails of a rat?'

'More than an omen, Lomgo, more than an omen. ... A promise. ... The promise of fulfilment ...'

The scribe knitted his brow. 'I don't understand, Master.'

'It doesn't matter, it doesn't matter ... I'm used to it ... I understand on behalf of those who don't understand. ... You just concentrate on writing and doing as I tell you.'

Lomgo pursed his lips. He had a fairly high opinion of himself and hated being humiliated in this way. However, he forced a smile and bowed his head. The Master was powerful. Very powerful. Perhaps even too powerful. With one hand, Lomgo placed a large blank sheet of paper on his desk. With the other, the one with the missing finger, he picked up a quill pen, dipped it in the ink and waited for the Master to begin dictating.

The letter written, Lomgo took his leave and made his exit. The form shrouded in shadows walked over to the door, closed and locked it, then went and stood in the centre of the room. There, he suddenly seemed to go wild, dancing, gesticulating and chanting a strange incantation. There was a flash of light, the room lit up and everything including the form and his shadow disappeared, as if sucked into the void.

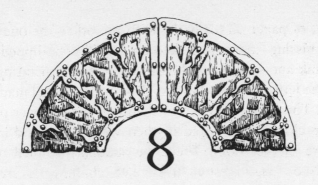

8

Secrets under the stars

'Master Quadehar,' said Robin as they were walking along the sea shore on a beach of grey sand, 'if you are a Sorcerer of the Guild, why don't you live in a monastery in a remote spot on the moors or in the mountains, like the others?'

Robin's initiation had begun. For the last month now he had been spending every free moment with the sorcerer, taking notes and trying to remember an incredible number of things, from the names of plants and types of seaweed to the position of the major ley lines – those invisible waves of energy that flow through the earth like ocean currents – and the main episodes in the history of the Guild. It was an impossibly daunting task, and Robin fell asleep exhausted every night. From time to time, they took a break from their work and set off in no particular direction, for the pure pleasure of walking. During those moments, the atmosphere was more relaxed and Robin made the most of it to try and satisfy his curiosity.

'Why, my boy?' replied Quadehar observing the flight of a seagull. 'Because I am a Pursuer. It's as simple as that!'

Robin stood open-mouthed. 'A Pursuer? But why have you never told me?'

'Probably because you've never asked me, Robin.'

The Pursuers were both sorcerers and knights who spent most of their time in The Uncertain World, pursuing individuals or other creatures who posed some sort of threat to The Lost Isle, and trying to render them harmless. The Pursuers were few in number, and there were all sorts of weird and wonderful stories about them. Robin couldn't believe that Master Quadehar was one of them!

'You must have seen some astounding things, Master Quadehar!'

The boy was staring at him round-eyed. The sorcerer was amused at Robin's excitement. 'Oh yes, I've seen some astounding things! Too many to be able to tell you about here and now. Later, if you work hard ...'

'Master,' implored Robin, 'please tell me a little.'

Quadehar seemed to waver, then gave in. 'Very well, Robin. But only the beginning, no more!'

They sat down on the sand, facing the ocean that sparkled under the rays of the setting sun. Robin was thrilled.

The sorcerer began: 'Back in those days, I was young and proud. I had decided to enter the Guild to become the new Tarquin, the sorcerer who would blow away the cobwebs from the old order and take it in a new direction! I studied hard and within a few years I reached a very respectable level of sorcery; I felt ready to take on the dark mantle and accomplish a thousand feats! But my master thought that, although I was a gifted magician, I was also too unruly and fond of fighting to make a good sorcerer. ... You see, Robin, calmness and self-control are two essential qualities for a good magician. In short, he didn't know what to do with me, and I was beginning to picture myself being doomed to remain an apprentice until my dying day. ... Then a young and brilliant sorcerer, newly ordained, vanished with the Guild's most precious work – the *Book of the Stars* – which was kept under lock and key at the monastery of Gifdu. This unique and ancient book of spells contains secrets that only the Magi, the wisest sorcerers, are allowed to read. It was believed that the thief had fled to The Uncertain World. In those days, there were no Pursuers left in the Guild, and they were reluctant to ask for the help of the Brotherhood of Knights who still had a few brave chosen souls. So they asked for volunteer sorcerers to follow the traitor to The Uncertain World, hunt him down and reclaim the famous book. I offered immediately, as you can imagine! I was accepted; the thief had been in the same year as me, he had even been in the same class and they thought that knowing him might give me an advantage. ... That's the beginning of my tale, my boy. That's how I became a Pursuer.'

And on that note, Quadehar rose to show that he had finished his story.

'What happened next?' asked Robin impatiently.

'I said I'd tell you the beginning, no more. I'll tell you the rest another time.'

'Just tell me, Master,' pleaded Robin, 'who that sorcerer was and whether you caught him.'

'His name was Yorwan. And nobody has ever found him. Don't ask me any more. The subject is closed for today.'

Robin understood from his Master's curt tone that there was no point questioning him further. Disappointed, he kicked a pebble.

Quadehar's expression had become serious again. 'My boy, you've been working with me for four weeks now. Tell me the truth, do you regret your decision?'

'No, Master Quadehar,' replied Robin looking him straight in the eye. 'But ... it's just that ...'

'Tell me, I asked you to be honest.'

Robin sighed then took his courage in both hands. 'It's just that sometimes I feel as if I'm not cut out to be a magician. I get the names of the flowers muddled up, I can't sense the ley lines and I fall asleep during the concentration exercises. Are you sure that I really had a Tarquin reaction?'

Quadehar laughed out loud and placed his hands on Robin's shoulders. 'It's quite natural, Robin. You have only been my pupil for a month! It takes three years to complete an apprenticeship, another three years to become a fully fledged sorcerer and a whole lifetime to merit that title! I think you're doing absolutely fine.'

'Really?' asked Robin, with a hopeful smile.

'Really! Think about the story I've just told you. What

lessons can be learned from it?'

Robin pondered for a moment, then ventured, 'That you have to be patient and wait ... for destiny to give you a sign?'

'Well done, Robin,' said Quadehar proudly. 'That you have to wait, learn and work, and your time will come!'

They set off on the path home. It was beginning to get dark.

'How are things with your mother and your uncle?' asked the sorcerer.

'OK,' replied Robin evasively. 'It might seem odd, but my mother seems thrilled that I've become an apprentice, though Uncle Urian doesn't seem so pleased. But I'm used to that; whatever I do, it's never good enough for him.'

'You don't seem to like your uncle very much, Robin.'

'He's the one who doesn't like me very much.'

Quadehar smiled. 'That's an honest answer. And how's school?' he went on, still walking, his hands clasped behind his back.

'So-so. It's not great, what with the teachers giving us loads of tests and this half-crazy girl who's always bullying me! But I get by.'

The sorcerer placed his hand on Robin's shoulder again. 'You're brave, Robin. I knew that as soon as you rushed at me, sword in hand, when I came into your room. That's good! Courage, determination and integrity are the three qualities a person needs to discover the best in themselves!'

Then Quadehar gazed up at the sky. 'Look, Robin. ...'

The deep-blue sky was studded with hundreds of stars.

'Can you recognize the stars, my boy?'

'Of course I can! We studied the map of the sky last year,' replied Robin, craning his neck to try and pick out the Great Bear. 'That was easy! But this year, we're doing the winds, and they're not so straightforward. ... Found it! There's the Great Bear. From there I can identify all the others.'

'The Pleiades. ... The Dolphin. ... And the Lyre. ... And over there, look, there's the Northern Crown!'

'That's good,' said Quadehar. Then he added, as if changing the subject, 'You see, Robin, the Guild began with the *Book of the Stars*. That book contains many secrets, most of which are incomprehensible even for the cleverest sorcerers! But, above all, it contains the basis of our magic. Anyone can learn the names of the flowers or the map of elementary forces if they make the effort. But magic, the ability to act on things – for example, strengthening the power of a herbal brew, creating a mist or turning metal into dust – needs special powers! It's these powers that are found in the *Book of the Stars* ... I promise I'll tell you more about it very soon.'

'When, Master, when?' exclaimed Robin, sensing that the sorcerer had touched on a very important subject which was much more exciting than all the complicated plant names he'd had to learn.

'The master usually shows his pupil the *Book of the Stars* at the end of the first year of his apprenticeship. I think you are gifted, Robin; we will open it at the end of your third month.'

'But how come?' asked Robin, puzzled. 'You told me that the *Book of the Stars* had been stolen by this Yorwan. ...'

'Centuries ago, the Guild took from this book everything it could understand,' Quadehar reassured him. 'These teachings have been handed down for generations, from the sorcerers to their apprentices! In the meantime, I want you to learn all there is to know about the plants growing on the hillsides and the ley lines around Penmarch.'

Robin promised to do everything that the sorcerer demanded. Things were suddenly beginning to get interesting!

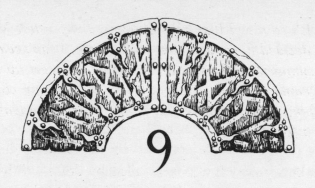

9

A question of flower names

Dear Robin,

Thank you for your letter. Your news is unbelievable! So you're an apprentice sorcerer! And not to any old sorcerer: Quadehar the Pursuer! I asked my father – Quadehar's a celebrity. People say he's spent his life tracking down monsters of all kinds, and he's said to be the only man that The Shadow fears. ...

Robin paused. Was Godfrey right? So, The Shadow, the great menace from The Uncertain World, the sworn enemy of the people of The Lost Isle, evil and elusive, who had ravaged the island on several occasions, was fearful of his master? That explained the fact that, at Uncle Urian's, the sorcerer had dared evoke The Shadow publicly, without seeming the slightest bit afraid.

He went back to the letter.

...It's so weird that he's become a baby-sitter! Maybe he's decided to settle down. In any case, I can't wait for the summer holidays. It'll be great to all meet up again in Penmarch! OK, I've got to go now. Your cousin's jumping up and down next to me because he wants to add a few words.

Robin broke off again, assailed by doubts. Why had Quadehar chosen him of all people? Was his master right urging him to abandon his dream of becoming a knight to enter into the service of the Guild? He couldn't help feeling anxious about it, often wondering whether he had made the right decision.

Deep down, even when he hoped with all his heart that he had found his calling, he was convinced that the sorcerer was mistaken about him, and that he had no special talent for magic at all.

If he was average at everything else, why should it be different with sorcery? But it was too late to change his mind – he could never be a knight now. At best, he was free to give up his apprenticeship and live an ordinary life as a citizen of The Lost Isle. But that didn't appeal to him at all. He preferred to think that, even if he wasn't especially gifted, he could become some sort of sorcerer if he worked hard! Until destiny gave him a sign, as it had given his Master.

He went back to the letter again.

Dear cousin Robin,
I'm pushing that prat Godfrey out of the way –

honestly he's been so full of himself since he played at Uncle Urian's party – to tell you that I'm very proud that you've been singled out by the great Quadehar! My father thinks it's a stupid idea and that our uncle should never have given his permission. Of course I defended you!

Result: no cinema on Saturday. I can't wait to be a knight, so you and I can go hunting down monsters in The Uncertain World! Anyway, we'll be meeting up soon. Amber wrote and told me that she and Coral are definitely coming to spend the holidays in Penmarch. It's going to be fantastic!

Love,
Romaric

In a daze, Robin tucked the letter away in his bag. It was true, the summer holidays weren't far off. He had swotted like mad this term so as to be sure of doing well in his exams. But, above all, he had studied hard with Quadehar. He was ready. This evening, his master would at last show him the *Book of the Stars*!

Sitting on a bench in the playground, deep in thought, he wasn't aware that someone was coming towards him.

'So, Robin, daydreaming are you?'

Robin jumped. In front of him Agatha Balangru and her gang stood eyeing him with a mixture of hostility and curiosity.

'Don't frighten him,' sneered one of the boys. 'He might faint!'

They all sniggered. The tall girl pulled a wry face and

silenced them with a wave of her hand.

'True, is it, shorty? Some sorcerer's taken you on as his apprentice?'

Robin watched Agatha carefully and thought fast. Despite her scornful air, she wasn't behaving with her usual arrogance. It was almost as if ... almost as if she were afraid! But afraid of what, or who? Of him, it was obvious! Or rather of the apprentice sorcerer he now was. Robin's heart began to race. This was his moment! He wouldn't get another opportunity like this.

He got up and tried to remain calm.

'Yes, it's true. Quadehar the Sorcerer is teaching me magic.'

He had uttered his master's name in the hope they'd be intimidated – and they were. There was a muttering from the gang. Agatha silenced them again, but she now seemed downright hesitant.

Robin had to seize his chance, before she regained her confidence. He looked them all up and down, and announced boldly, in a calm voice, 'Yesterday, Master Quadehar taught me a good trick: how to shrink people's legs! I'll show you.'

Robin struck the same attitude that Quadehar had adopted to turn the swords to dust, and uttered in a powerful voice, '*Taraxacum! Papaver rhoeas!*'

Thomas Kandarisar, as stupid as he was strong, let out a howl and ran off as fast as his legs would carry him, the rest of the gang hot on his heels. Agatha shot a look of hatred at the skinny boy who stood with his arms raised to the heavens invoking evil powers, then she too fled.

Robin burst out laughing. He'd just frightened the wits out of the school bullies by yelling the botanical names of the dandelion and poppy! For that moment of pure satisfaction, he would never regret having said yes to Quadehar! Magic was fun.

As it was getting late, Robin left the school grounds, walked through the town and set off down the road to Penmarch, hurrying towards the hill where he was meeting Quadehar.

A giant dolmen stood on the hill top, from which there was a magnificent view of the sea to the south, and the mountains to the east. The children from the town loved coming to play here, and it was a favourite haunt of lovers in the spring, when there was a full moon. But today, Robin was here for a different reason.

Quadehar was waiting for him, sitting cross-legged on the giant granite slab. He rose to greet him. 'Hello, Robin!'

'Hello, Master,' replied the boy, breathless from the walk.

'The air smells wonderful,' said Quadehar, taking a deep breath, 'Don't you think?'

'Yes,' faltered Robin who had not been expecting such a casual greeting.

'I love this place! It really does have something magical about it!'

The sorcerer's tone told Robin that he was leading up to something. The apprentice took his cue from his master. 'Naturally, Master, the Penmarch ley lines meet the Dashtikazar ley lines here.'

Quadehar gave him a shrewd look. 'Remind me what ley lines are, Robin,' he asked abruptly, suddenly changing his tone.

'An invisible energy current that flows through the earth, Master. From time to time, several ley lines join up and form a huge source of energy. The places where they meet are called nexus points. They are very powerful. This is one, Master.'

Robin had replied with perfect assurance.

Quadehar jumped off the dolmen, bent over amid the plants and plucked a flower which he held under Robin's nose. 'What's this?'

'*Hypericum maculatum*, Imperforate St-John's wort!' It should be picked in summer. It contains an oil that turns red and is used for healing cuts and sores.'

'Is it the only plant of its kind?'

Robin hesitated, until Quadehar glared at him, then he stammered, 'Er, no, no ... it has a sister, *Hypericum perforatum*, Perforate St-John's wort, which prefers dryer soil.'

The sorcerer's face lit up with a big smile. 'Good, Robin, very good!' He clambered back onto the dolmen and signalled to the boy to come and join him. 'You've worked very hard. Besides, I've never doubted your abilities.'

Robin glowed with pride.

His master went on, 'As I promised, I'm going to show you the *Book of the Stars* and teach you the secrets of the Guild. But first, I have a present for you.'

From his magician's sack, he took out a brand new

canvas bag and a thick black leather-bound notebook.

'Every apprentice sorcerer has a bag like this, in which he keeps his books, the plants he gathers and ... his own personal notebook, in which he records his progress and his own discoveries.'

Robin took the two objects with the greatest care and examined them delightedly.

'I will never check what you write in your notebook, Robin,' added Quadehar, amused by his pupil's reaction. 'It's up to you to decided what's worth recording in it.'

'Thank you very much, Master! They're the best presents anyone's ever given me!'

'Good, good,' the sorcerer replied softly, moved by the boy's answer. 'Are you ready now for the *Book of the Stars?*'

'Oh yes,' replied Robin, his eyes shining. 'I'm ready!'

'Well, listen to me, and if there's something you don't understand, don't hesitate to stop me and ask questions.'

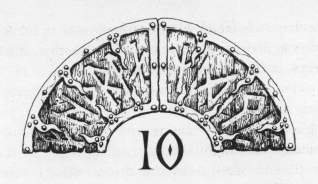

10

The secret of the night

'Robin, my young pupil,' began Quadehar, 'the first thing you have to learn in order to gain access to the magic understanding of the world, is how to look at it differently. You must recognize this stone,' he went on, pointing to a rock, 'feel this wind,' he said, filling his lungs, 'hear that bird song. At first, they seem to have nothing in common. But in fact there is something that links them all!'

'Something, Master?' queried Robin determined to try and grasp fully the secret of magic which Quadehar was disclosing to him.

'Yes, Robin, an invisible bond which unites every living thing. In other words all the five elements. You know the five elements, I hope?'

'I, er ...' stammered Robin, 'I thought there were only four: fire, earth, air and water.'

'You're forgetting flesh!' chided Quadehar mischievously.

'Flesh. ... You mean meat?'

'I mean people, plants, animals. ... Everything that breathes, my boy! Do you follow? Shall I go on?'

'Yes, yes, Master. Go on!'

'Well, these five elements are joined by an invisible, intangible link, which our ancestors called the Wyrd. Remember: the Wyrd! Like a giant spider's web whose threads are attached to each and every thing. What do you think of that?'

'I see,' said Robin cautiously. 'That would mean that, for example, if I move, the whole web moves, and the whole world would feel me moving. ... Impossible. ...'

'No, Robin,' replied Quadehar visibly delighted by his pupil's reply, 'not impossible. It's just that the web is so vast that when you move, nobody and nothing feels it directly, other than those really close to you. The mathematicians of The Real World had some idea of the Wyrd and based the Chaos Theory on it. Have you heard of the Chaos Theory?'

'Er ...' mumbled Robin, 'yes, I think so. Isn't it that the thing about a butterfly's wing beating and causing a storm on the other side of the planet?'

'That's right – to put it in a nutshell, the Chaos Theory says that even a tiny little insignificant act can have an effect on everything else. Now,' went on the sorcerer, 'supposing we were able to control those effects. That we could act with the knowledge of what the effect would be at a *precise* point in the web.'

'That would mean,' said Robin slowly, 'that we would have the power to influence things through other things that, at first glance, seem to have nothing to do with each other. ... But how, Master?'

Quadehar smiled at the boy's sudden excitement as the full extent of the secret of the Guild opened up to him.

'Through keys, Robin. Keys that make it possible to enter the Wyrd, to reach the innermost structure of life!'

'Keys? Like keys that open doors?' suggested the apprentice timidly.

'Precisely, my boy! Except that these keys aren't things you hold in your hand, but signs.'

The sorcerer stretched his long body and sighed contentedly, enjoying the last rays of sunshine. He had a distant look in his eyes for a moment, as he gazed towards the horizon.

Robin tugged the sleeve of his dark cloak and implored, 'Master Quadehar, please. ...'

Quadehar laughed affectionately. 'Are you developing a taste for the secrets of sorcery, Robin?'

'You were talking about signs, Master,' urged the boy, 'signs that allow you to open doors!'

'Yes,' went on the sorcerer with pleasure, watching Robin carefully write, word for word, everything he said in his brand new notebook. 'Think of it like a sort of alphabet, where each letter has a particular meaning and a special power. Now, think of those letters being joined together in words, then the words linked to other words in sentences. And now you have the necessary energy to visualize, enter and modify the Wyrd. That is the secret, Robin, the secret of magic – establishing and controlling a link between things that are very different!'

'Brilliant!' exclaimed Robin. 'That means that with these signs, you can control the universe!'

'Not so fast,' smiled Quadehar at his apprentice's enthusiasm. 'It's not quite so simple. First of all, sorcery isn't an exact science, but the outcome of continual trial and error and experimentation. Then, the Wyrd has its own laws which must not be broken, otherwise the whole thing will collapse. And lastly, these signs, which we sorcerers call Graphems, are neutral energies whose effect depends solely on the person using them. ... What do you make of that, Robin?'

'Er ... that you need to be careful? And think about what you're doing?'

'Well done!' replied Quadehar, looking pleased and clapping the boy on the shoulder. 'Until you reach the age of wisdom, prudence and humility must be the sorcerer's watchwords.'

'Tell me more about the signs ... about the Graphems, Master.'

'Robin, first of all I'm going to tell you more about what you'll be studying in the next few years. And if that doesn't put you off, then I'll tell you more about the Graphems.'

'All right!' agreed Robin, thrilled.

'You're going to have to work very hard at subjects that will seem to you to have little to do with magic proper, such as geology, geography and history. Learn the wind charts, the ley lines and the ocean currents, the composition of rocks and metals, animal behaviour, the properties of plants, human psychology – in other words, everything to do with the five elements – because an in-depth understanding of the world is crucial for anyone who wants to influence the Wyrd.'

Robin sighed. Magic suddenly seemed a lot less fun than he had imagined. Still, he nodded.

Quadehar went on, 'You will do exercises to strengthen your body and keep it supple. Magic needs power and endurance. You will work at your breathing. Breath is the driving force behind magic. Never neglect your body, Robin; it is your only source of energy.'

'Does a sorcerer's strength depend on his body, Master?' asked Robin anxiously.

'Yes and no, my boy. A sorcerer's strength resides above all in the way in which he masters his art – but also in his ability to use elementary energies; and you need to be tough to channel a flow of energy from the earth, believe me! Some sorcerers have a higher degree than others of the special inner strength that we call 'Ond' and that gives our magic its power. A powerful Ond is something you are born with, in the same way that some people can run fast or others are good at drawing.'

'This ... Ond, Master,' ventured Robin. 'Does it have anything to do with the Tarquin effect?'

'It could,' replied Quadehar. 'As always, I see you grasp things quickly. Shall I go on?'

Robin nodded vigorously.

The sorcerer continued. 'While you're training your memory and your body, you will work on the Graphems. First of all, you must get to know them well – their names, their shapes, their alphabetical order and their powers. Then, you must absorb them, rediscover them for yourself through meditation, hold them in your heart and in your mind. Once you have acquired the Graphems, I will help you learn to write or engrave them, sing them, call them up and replicate them. They will enable you to defend yourself against all assailants and to overpower any adversary, or to see into and even predict the future! What do you think of what you have learnt so far?'

Robin remained silent for a moment. What he thought was that he clearly had no real choice. And that this part of the programme sounded really difficult. Still, he mustered his enthusiasm and concentrated on the mysterious Graphems which fascinated him. 'Brilliant, Master!'

'Good, good, my boy. What would you like to know now?'

'These Graphems ... Who invented them?'

'Nobody knows who invented them, Robin. No more than we know who wrote the *Book of the Stars*, nor even how long it has been in our possession. ... It was through this book that we learned about the Graphems, although we know they have always been within human grasp.

'Where, Master, where?' asked Robin looking about him eagerly.

'Why ... up there, my boy,' the sorcerer answered gently, pointing to the stars that were gradually lighting up the sky as the dusk deepened, melting into the secrecy of night.

'You mean ...'

'I simply mean that the Graphems come to us from the stars, or rather from certain constellations whose form they imitate. That's why we called our book of spells the *Book of the Stars* – because of the night sky and the alphabet of lighted dots formed by the stars, echoing the Wyrd itself.'

Suddenly, Robin was overjoyed – his doubts melted away as his gaze roamed the sky. He felt as though he had found his place in the world at last – up there, among the stars!

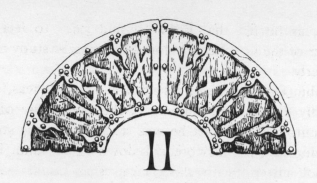

II

Kidnapped

Robin, his eyes shut tight, was trying to picture the third Graphem of the Star alphabet. Although it was a simple shape, he was having difficulty seeing it in his mind. He made a final attempt to concentrate but failed. He abandoned the exercise and opened his eyes. He blinked in the harsh noon sunlight that was reflected off the sandy beach where he had come to work.

The pressure of school work had eased off as the summer holidays approached. It was now three weeks since Quadehar, Master Sorcerer, had opened the *Book of the Stars* for him and, ever since, he had been trying to memorize the symbols described in it, the keys that opened the doors to the world of magic. He'd spent nearly the whole three weeks on the first three Graphems, neglecting the five elements. And what was the result? The three little shapes still had to be coaxed to appear when he closed his eyes. His master had given him only the shapes and the names of the twenty-four signs, as he felt that Robin should learn to feel the power of the Graphems before beginning to study them properly.

Robin felt a surge of resentment. Here he was, supposedly the talented apprentice, chosen because of the Tarquin effect, and yet he was stuck over some stupid drawings! He put his notebook down on the sand. Then he took a deep breath, closed his eyes again and concentrated as hard as he could. The first Graphem appeared a little fuzzily in his blank mind: Fehu, which reminded him for some reason of a big fat cow. The second emerged alongside the first: Uruz, which made him think of rain. And lastly, the third appeared next to it – Thursaz, which seemed to be laughing like his uncle, with a giant's guffaw. This time, he'd succeeded! He was elated.

Just then, a voice broke into his thoughts, 'Do you think he's asleep? Hey, dozy, are you asleep?'

Robin shuddered as he recognized the voice of Thomas Kandarisar. He opened his eyes – it wasn't a dream; the redheaded bully was sitting on the sand opposite him and, next to him, with her hands on her hips and a nasty sneer on her face, towered Agatha Balangru. Drat! He thought he'd managed to shake Agatha and her gang off with his pretend magic words.

'We need to talk, midget,' snarled Agatha who no longer seemed afraid of him.

'Yeah,' grunted Thomas, 'you really tried to make us look stupid with your fake spells.'

'Don't deny it, shorty,' Agatha went on, 'I asked my

father. He told me that an apprentice can't do magic.'

'Yeah, too dumb!' added Thomas. 'It's s'posed to take years before you can do spells!'

'So we thought,' finished Agatha in a threatening voice, 'that we should check it out for ourselves. Go on Thomas!'

Thomas lunged at Robin, who had leaped to his feet ready to take to his heels and run. But that would have meant abandoning his precious notebook; so he stayed put and braced himself for the blow.

But the blow didn't come, for Thomas was frozen to the spot, seemingly petrified, his eyes bulging as he stared at the sea. Agatha turned to follow his gaze and screamed in terror. Two Gommons had risen out of the water and were making straight for them!

The Gommons, huge creatures with glassy eyes, hair of seaweed and a skin of slimy scales, were like men in appearance but more like animals in their behaviour ... ferocious animals. Equally at home in the water, on the sand or among the rocks where they lived, they had shown themselves in the past to be a fisherman's worst enemies. And so, a few centuries back, they had been exiled to The Uncertain World, as a result of a joint action by the Guild and the Brotherhood. Since then, the people of The Lost Isle only knew about them from books and legends.

However, the Gommons rushing towards them at that moment were, without a doubt, horribly real.

'Run! Run, Agatha!' yelled Thomas as Agatha stood rigid with terror, unable to move a muscle.

Cursing, the boy grabbed her arm and dragged her along, following Robin who shouted at them to hurry. The three of them made for the grassy dunes, where the ground was firmer and they had a chance of throwing the Gommons off.

Robin ran as fast as he could, but within minutes he was beginning to feel out of breath. His feet sank into the sand, and the simple action of putting one foot in front of the other was exhausting. He had the unpleasant sense that every stride he took was pulling him backwards. It was like his worst nightmare – being chased by a monster but finding his feet glued to the ground, preventing him from running away. Robin was trembling all over. He'd never make it to the dunes at this rate! He glanced back; Thomas and Agatha weren't faring any better, they seemed to be finding it even more difficult. The two monsters were gaining steadily on them.

Thomas turned around, the scaly creatures were now just a few steps behind them. He panicked and shouted out. And in that split second he let go of Agatha's arm so he could move faster. This threw Agatha off balance and she stumbled and fell. A moment later, the first Gommon was upon her. Agatha shrieked and thrashed about frantically. But it was useless. She was immobilized in a powerful grip. Effortlessly, the monster lifted her up, flung her over its shoulder and carried her off towards the ocean, heedless of its victim's cries and shouts for help. Now, the second Gommon was lumbering towards the two boys who had stopped running, frozen to the spot by the terrible scene they had just witnessed. The monster grinned unpleasantly, revealing vicious sharp teeth. The gleaming knife it held left them in no doubt as to its intentions; they were not going to be kidnapped, but killed!

'AAAAAAGH!' They both let out a shriek of terror and bolted.

'Faster! Faster!' panted Robin as Thomas fell behind.

Unlike the children, the Gommon was used to moving across sand and was quickly close on their heels. They were almost at the dunes. They might still make it, but only by a hair's breadth! At that moment Thomas tripped and doubled up on the sand, groaning in pain.

Robin, stopped in his tracks by the cry, urged his companion on. 'Get up, Thomas! Come on. Up!'

The boy lay on the ground his eyes wide with terror as their pursuer drew nearer by the second. He tried to get up, but his ankle gave way. He appeared to have sprained it, as he collapsed in his attempt to put weight on his foot.

'I can't,' moaned Thomas. 'Go on, run!'

Robin hesitated. He was sure he could shake off the Gommon once he reached the grassy dunes. The first houses were only ten minutes away; he could get help quickly. But not quickly enough to save Thomas. He'd wished him dead a thousand times when the redhead had bullied him at school, but it was one thing wishing someone dead when you were angry, and quite another to have it really happen! The grim fate awaiting Thomas was far worse than his taunting of Robin. No, he'd fight beside the boy to the end, and he wouldn't abandon him. No matter what happened! There was no getting away from your true nature, thought Robin. Becoming an apprentice sorcerer may have taught him caution, but he still believed in showing the courage of a true knight!

The Gommon was now less than a metre away: there was no point trying to flee. Beside himself with fear, Thomas Kandarisar, helped by Robin, crawled along the ground clutching his ankle, in a final bid to escape. Now, the creature just had to reach out to catch hold of him. It knew it, and appeared to be taking its time, perhaps relishing the sport of the chase. The blade of the knife it was holding glinted in the sunlight.

Then, something truly extraordinary happened.

In Robin's head, the third Graphem suddenly appeared of its own accord, much more clearly than when he had been practising. The sign quickly filled his mind, grew and caught fire, spreading within him a heat that was at first gentle, but which soon became unbearable. It felt as though he was being consumed from within by the Graphem. He let go of Thomas and stood up to confront their pursuer. Holding his head in his hands and groaning, Robin writhed with pain.

Taken aback, the Gommon froze and stared at him with glassy eyes.

Then, without thinking, Robin shouted the name of the Graphem. Somehow, it seemed to him like the only way to stop the pain. 'THUUURSAAAAZ!!!!'

The Gommon recoiled abruptly as if it had been punched violently in the stomach. It moaned, gazed at the two boys in astonishment then crumpled in a heap on the sand.

There was a moment's astounded silence, then Thomas struggled to his feet. 'Wow! How did you do that?' he exclaimed.

Robin had immediately felt relief from the burning fire after shouting the name of the Graphem. It was as though the magic sign had appeared on its own to show him what to do, for he had acted completely without thinking! He and Thomas stared at the unconscious Gommon on the ground, unable to believe their eyes.

'How did you do that, tell me, how did you do it?' repeated Thomas in a quivering voice, full of admiration.

Robin's legs were still like jelly. He had never been so scared in his whole life! Not even the time when his Uncle Urian had chased him through Penmarch Castle to give him a whipping because he and Romaric had slipped a dead rat into his bed. ...

He paused and drew a deep breath before answering, 'I'm learning sorcery. ... Didn't I tell you?'

Thomas Kandarisar was dumbstruck and merely nodded solemnly. Then they suddenly remembered Agatha had been snatched. In their joy at still being alive, the boys had forgotten all about her, and now the full horror of the situation came flooding back.

'We must hurry and inform the Brotherhood straight away,' said Robin to Thomas, who was still in shock. Still thinking about Agatha's disappearance, Thomas was unable to stifle a sob.

Robin retraced his steps to the place where he had left

his notebook on the sand and stuffed it into his bag.
Then, with a heavy, limping Thomas leaning on Robin
for support, the two boys set out towards Dashtikazar.

12

In the Provost's palace

Agatha's kidnapping caused a great stir. Or rather it caused something of an earthquake that shook the whole of The Lost Isle. Mr Balangru kicked up a stink over his daughter's disappearance and railed against the Brotherhood, which he claimed hadn't done its job in protecting the population. The Brotherhood left no stone unturned in their hunt for the missing girl, but their search proved fruitless. And there was also great consternation because the presence of Gommons on the coast meant that The Lost Isle was no longer safe from the dangers of The Uncertain World. What everyone feared most was that The Shadow was behind this latest provocation.

The people of The Lost Isle had good reason to remember The Shadow's previous attacks – from the destruction of entire villages by gangs of bloodthirsty Orks (the land equivalent of the Gommons, except that they were a pure product of The Uncertain World) to the almost successful attempt to burn down Dashtikazar with fireballs. And on both occasions the knights and sorcerers had come within a whisker of being defeated.

The Lost Isle was in a turmoil. The clans held an assembly and, in every district, village and hamlet, the men took turns to keep watch. The roads and the paths echoed to the sound of galloping hooves as the Knights of the Brotherhood scoured the land. People hadn't seen so many dark cloaks combing the towns and countryside for a long time.

Today was a special day, no longer because it was the first day of the summer holidays, but because the Provost had convened a meeting of the highest powers – the representatives of the clans, the Chief Sorcerer of the Guild, the Commander of the Brotherhood and the delegate of the tradesmen's and craftsmen's corporations. The inhabitants of The Lost Isle had high hopes for this meeting of the great and the good.

'Well, my boy, how are you?' Master Quadehar asked Robin as the two of them walked down a long corridor in the Provost's Palace, leading to the council chamber.

'I'll feel better when this is over,' replied Robin pulling a face.

Being summoned by the Provost along with the leading dignitaries of The Lost Isle was enough to intimidate even the boldest of boys! Robin had only accepted the invitation on the assurance that he could be accompanied by his master.

'Bah!' replied Quadehar, flashing him one of his encouraging smiles. 'After what you've been through, this meeting will be a piece of cake!'

'Yeah, right' grumbled Robin, 'I still think I'd rather come face to face with a whole gang of Gommons.'

Quadehar hooted with laughter, and Robin soon joined in. Since the day on the beach when he had vanquished the monster from the sea, he had become a hero for all the people of The Lost Isle, except in the eyes of Agatha's father who had even criticized him outright for not saving his daughter. And his Uncle Urian, of course, who had merely grunted that he'd been lucky to get away with his life and that there was nothing to make a fuss about.

Once over the shock, his mother had reacted with a mixture of pride and anxiety. But the person who had been most affected by this episode was Thomas. Since Robin had snatched him from the clutches of the Gommon, the Kandarisar boy gazed at him with blind admiration and followed him everywhere, just as he had followed Agatha before. At first, this had irritated Robin. Then, seeing there was nothing he could do about it, he had grown used to it.

They reached the council chamber. Quadehar knocked on the huge, solid-oak door. A guard opened it and bade them enter. Sitting around an imposing circular table, facing them, were the Provost and his distinguished guests.

'Good day, good day, Master Quadehar, it is always a pleasure to see you!' the great man greeted the sorcerer.

The Provost was a man in his seventies, with eagle eyes and a confident voice. In his day, he had been a just and righteous clan chief, and he had been elected to this position with a comfortable majority, as he was reputed to be astute in business matters and a skilful diplomat, open to advice but firm in his decisions. So far, the people of The Lost Isle had been delighted with their choice.

'Your Honour,' replied Quadehar giving a slight bow, while Robin hung back trying to remain unnoticed.

Seated around the table was also the commander in charge of the Brotherhood, a huge man in his prime, whose face bore the scars of countless battles. He had been the best knight of his generation, and his peers had been unanimous in electing him. His predecessor had been slain during the bloody battles in the Golden Mountains against the hordes of Orks sent by The Shadow.

Beside him sat a pot-bellied man with a keen gaze, the elected representative of the craftsmen and tradesmen. Although less illustrious than the other four, he perhaps held the most real power, for he was the spokesman for the corporations on which the entire country depended for its survival. He was frequently at loggerheads with the Provost over the products that The Lost Isle imported from The Real World, but that was the name of the game, and their disagreements were only natural.

The next man was a familiar face. There, giving Robin a friendly wave, was Utigern Krakal, Amber and Coral's father, the elected representative of the Qamdars. He was a smallish, slim man, with brown hair. His most striking feature were his blue eyes, which his daughters had inherited. Of all those present, he was the one whose authority was most questionable, as a result of the rivalries that divided the clans.

Lastly, at the end of the table, wearing a dark, hooded cloak, was Charfalaq, the Chief Sorcerer of the Guild, an emaciated old man who was almost blind and had to strain his eyes in the direction of whoever was speaking. 'Don't be taken in by his appearance,' Quadehar had warned him, 'despite his great age, our Chief Sorcerer is still very powerful.'

'Ah! This must be Robin Penmarch, the hero who fought the Gommons,' said the Provost turning towards the boy. 'Come closer. Don't be afraid.'

As Robin came shyly forward, the Provost spoke to Utigern Krakal, whose friendly exchange with Robin had caught his eye, 'Do you know this young man, Utigern?'

'Of course, Your Honour. You'd have to be deaf not to have heard about him in my house!' Then he added, winking at Robin, 'he seems to be very popular with the girls of The Lost Isle.'

Everyone smiled, despite the gravity of the occasion. Robin turned scarlet, desperately wishing he knew the magic words – if they existed – that could make the earth swallow him up. He was sure this was some silly joke of Amber's, who must have twisted the story of his battles with Agatha and told her father this nonsense! He promised himself he'd sort her out the next time they met.

The Provost looked grave again and questioned Quadehar, 'Do we know how this boy was able to put a spell on the Gommon?'

'Not exactly, Your Honour,' replied the sorcerer, after

a quick glance in the direction of the Chief Sorcerer. 'It seems that Robin has a certain talent for magic, sufficient in any case to have triggered the Tarquin effect originally. I would suggest that fear combined with his receptive nature heightened his rudimentary powers of sorcery.'

The Provost turned to the Commander. 'Commander, is there any news of the Balangru girl?'

'I'm afraid not, Your Honour,' replied the knight. 'One thing is certain, however. She is no longer on The Lost Isle.'

The big man's reply was greeted with silence.

The Provost addressed the Chief Sorcerer. 'Chief Sorcerer Charfalaq, what progress have you made in your investigation? Has the captive Gommon revealed anything?'

'It is too soon, Your Honour,' replied the old man in a croaky, although steady, voice, interrupted by long fits of coughing. 'Our best sorcerers are working on this mystery. As for the Gommon. ... He's tough. But he'll crack eventually.'

Another silence followed the wise old man's words. It was broken by the trades- and craftsmen's representative, 'Do we have any idea why the Balangru girl was kidnapped? Has there been a ransom demand?'

'No,' replied the Commander, who was responsible for national security.

'But for heaven's sake!' exploded Utigern Krakal, 'What are we supposed to do? Our fellow citizens are terrified, they expect us to come up with some answers.'

'There's nothing else to be done,' the Provost replied

quietly. 'We must remain on our guard and wait for the results of the investigation ...'

'... or the next kidnapping!' bellowed the clan representative. 'I have two daughters, and you have children too, grandchildren even! I don't know about you, but I don't want to stand idly by while they're in danger!'

'Calm down, Utigern,' went on the Provost. 'Nobody wants any more kidnappings. But, as I said, we must be patient. Right now, we have other concerns. You, for example,' he added, turning to Robin.

'Me?' he stammered, 'But why? What have I done?'

'You are one of the only witnesses to the kidnapping,' explained the Commander. 'And it was you who defeated the second Gommon. His companion might have seen you. In any case, we must get you to a safe place quickly. One of the forts belonging to the Brotherhood, for example.'

The Chief Sorcerer raised his hand to signal that he wished to speak. Robin and the others, turned towards him. The old man had a special aura, and the apprentice immediately understood what his master had meant when he'd told him not to be taken in by appearances. The Chief Sorcerer looked as if his body took sustenance from magic, rather than magic taking sustenance from his body! Despite his instinctive dislike of this serious old man, Robin could not help feeling a certain respect and even admiration for him.

'Why not hide him in one of our monasteries?' suggested Charfalaq. 'There's no better protection.'

That was what Robin was afraid of. Being locked up

somewhere, just as summer was beginning! He pulled a face.

As if to reassure him, Quadehar placed a hand on his shoulder and asked for permission to speak. 'It's very kind of you to be so concerned for my pupil. ... However, I think that Robin will be safe enough with me. Let him stay in Penmarch. I'll stay there too and keep an eye on him, and at the same time we will continue our lessons.'

The members of the Council deliberated for a while, the Chief Sorcerer putting up the greatest opposition to Quadehar's proposal. Finally, the majority backed Quadehar's suggestion, which was deemed to be reasonable. After all, he was the one who was best acquainted with The Uncertain World and the creatures that lived there – and was even, so rumour had it, the only man capable of standing up to The Shadow, their dreaded enemy.

Quadehar noticed Robin's look of relief on hearing the Provost confirm the Council's decision to entrust him to his safekeeping, and gave him a knowing wink. Quadehar seemed to understand that Robin would want, more than anything, to spend the entire summer holidays at Penmarch with his friends, Romaric, Godfrey, Amber and Coral.

13

Together again

'Tell us about it again!' urged Romaric who was leaping about with excitement as Robin finished the story of his adventures for the tenth time.

'Oh, shut up,' replied Amber, 'can't you see he's had enough?'

'Oh, come on,' pleaded the fair-haired Romaric. 'It's not every day you get the chance to hear a real hero telling you about his exploits!'

'I can understand that,' chipped in Godfrey sarcastically. 'If I myself were a nobody, I'd feel the need to hang out with extraordinary people, like a Gommon slayer or a musical genius.'

'Yeah,' cried Romaric clapping tall, skinny Godfrey on the shoulder. 'Just you watch what a future knight is going to do to the musical genius!'

Just then, Coral opened the door to Robin's room, where they had taken refuge from the hot afternoon sun, carrying a tray with glasses of cool cola. They all cheered the arrival of the drinks, but Coral jokingly pretended to take the compliment for herself and danced around in delight, which looked so ridiculous it soon had them all shrieking with laughter.

The holidays were off to a brilliant start!

Since the gang had been reunited at Robin's house, they had happily passed the hours like this, laughing and teasing each other. They would have lost track of time altogether if Robin's mother hadn't called them down to meals.

This was the custom on The Lost Isle – during the school year, parents demanded a lot of their children but, in exchange, they allowed them almost total freedom during the two-month summer holidays. Needless to say, most schoolchildren spent the whole year looking forward to the end of the summer term!

The friends spent their time going for walks on the heath, or challenging each other to sports matches in Penmarch village square, playing cards in Robin's room or whiling away evenings in long discussions in the sitting room after watching a video.

Robin was often at the centre of the happy bunch. He had no objection to telling them what had happened over and over again; sometimes he found himself getting carried away, embroidering the story a little and swelling with pride on seeing his friends' shining eyes riveted to him. He had even caught a look of admiration in the gaze of his cousin Romaric, and that thrilled him perhaps more than anything else.

Today he was making the best of these moments, for

Quadehar, who was staying with Uncle Urian, had given him a whole day off. From tomorrow onwards he would have to spend part of every day with his master.

'Shall we walk to the cliffs?' suggested Amber after they had drained their glasses.

'Good idea,' agreed Godfrey leaping to his feet, quickly followed by the others.

They clattered down the stairs and out into the cobbled street that wound through the village of Penmarch.

Robin's house stood alone at the edge of the village. On one side stretched the heath, which ran down to the sea, and on the other was the beginning of an oak and beech forest, which ran deep into the countryside. The gang had opted for the cliffs, one of their favourite haunts.

Robin slowed down and soon found himself walking alongside Amber.

'Why did you tell your father all that stuff?'

'What stuff?' asked Amber with surprise, turning to face him.

'You know very well,' said Robin blushing crimson, 'about me and the girls of The Lost Isle. ...'

'Oh, that,' said Amber dismissively, 'I can't remember now. I suppose the idea came into my head and I thought it was funny!'

'Well, it wasn't funny at all,' muttered Robin.

Amber pretended to be surprised. 'What? So it's not true?'

Robin clammed up. You just couldn't have a serious

conversation with Amber.

Realizing she'd gone a bit too far, Amber tried to change the subject, 'It's really kind of your mother to have all four of us to stay for the whole two months!'

'Yes, it is,' agreed Robin, softening. 'She can't bear seeing me moping, which I would have done if I'd had to spend the summer away from you lot.'

'You creep!' teased Coral who had joined them, leaving Romaric gesticulating madly as he explained to Godfrey his training programme for his entrance exam for the Brotherhood.

'But I wish my mother was happier – sometimes I wonder if she feels guilty for letting my father leave and for not having given me any brothers or sisters,' sighed Robin.

'And to think I'd give anything to be an only child!' exclaimed Amber, while her sister glared daggers at her.

'The main thing is that she loves you, isn't it?' concluded Coral gently.

'Yes, yes, you're right,' said Robin evasively, chasing away any unpleasant thoughts of his father that might ruin this happy moment.

They soon came within sight of the white chalk cliffs. These fragile giants were slowly being eroded, their constantly changing features battered by the sea, wind and rain, whole sections eventually collapsing into the ocean below. They were less spectacular than those off the coast of the Bitter Moor or the Golden Mountains, the place where the split had occurred when the great storm had torn The Lost Isle from the mainland. But they were still awe-inspiring.

The friends took the path leading down to the pebble beach, after glancing at Robin, who reassured them. Just because Gommons had attacked him once, that was no reason to keep away from the beaches of The Lost Isle for ever.

On the way, Robin described to his amazed friends the wildlife that could be found on these seemingly bleak and inhospitable cliffs. When there was a gentle slope, there were green, grassy areas with red fescue and yarrow attracting butterflies and sometimes hedgehogs. The cracks in the sheer cliff face were a nesting place for seagulls, herring gulls and kestrels.

'Don't tell me you learned all that at school!' exclaimed Godfrey as they walked along the pebble shore.

'No, with Master Quadehar. ... It's part of my apprenticeship,' replied Robin.

'What about magic, then?' asked Coral inquisitively.

'I've told you,' he answered, 'I'm sworn to absolute secrecy, even with you. I promised ...'

'We know, we know,' grumbled Romaric. 'Coral wasn't thinking, that's all.

'She never does,' grumbled Amber, and then challenged them all – 'Let's go climbing! Who'll race me to the top of that rock?'

Her suggestion didn't meet with much enthusiasm. Nobody could climb as well as she could, and they knew it. As usual, Romaric was the only one to take her on.

'As if that would make him a better knight,' teased

Godfrey, as he and the other two sat down to watch the competition.

Romaric threw himself into the race, groaning with every movement. Amber climbed gracefully and nimbly, moving towards the top without any apparent effort. She seemed to be dancing on the cliff face, seeking hand- and footholds with supple, swinging movements. She was soon in the lead and it was not long before she reached the peak of the rock, to the cheers of the others down below. Although he still felt annoyed with her, Robin was impressed. For a fleeting moment, he found himself wondering if there was anything more inspiring than watching Amber bravely master a cliff face.

Panting and perspiring, Romaric finally caught up with her. She held out a hand to help him up the last metre, and he accepted gratefully. Sitting astride the rock, the pair of them waved their arms around and shouted triumphantly. Godfrey, Coral and Robin waved back to them.

Suddenly, Amber let out a screech. 'ROBIN! ROBIN! LOOK OUT!'

Deathly pale, she jumped up and down wildly gesticulating to a clump of bushes close to the sea. Romaric also began to shout and point. The three on the beach turned round sharply. On the pebbles not far from where they stood, they saw the broad shadow of a menacing form.

Coral began to shriek. Robin, rooted to the spot, tried for a second time to invoke the Graphem that had saved him before, but to no avail. Then, Thursaz had come to him unbidden, it wasn't he who had consciously called up the sign. He bowed his head, ashamed of having boasted to his friends but still determined to put up a fierce fight, despite everything. Then he saw Godfrey fish a strange whistle from his pocket with a trembling hand and blow into it fit to burst his lungs, although no sound emerged.

Suddenly, with a terrifying rumble and a burst of stars, a rock near where they stood apparently split open and from it emerged – *Quadehar!* He stumbled out and rushed between Robin and the shadow, which hadn't moved at all, immediately adopting a magic defence position. Time seemed to stand still. Nobody moved, or even dared to breathe.

A moment later, the sorcerer relaxed and burst out laughing. 'Come closer! Don't be afraid!'

From the bushes where he had hidden came the person whose shadow the sun had projected onto the beach.

'I'm not afraid,' muttered a voice they all recognized with amazement.

There, with his hands in his pockets and a look of annoyance, stood Thomas Kandarisar!

14

Hurray for the holidays!

'He's *so* clingy!' moaned Coral turning round and glimpsing Thomas's mop of red hair. He'd been following them at a distance.

'It's true,' agreed Romaric, 'but he's explained why he gave us such a scare on the beach the other day. He's sworn to keep watch over Robin to thank him for saving his life!'

'Had you lot noticed before that he was following me?' asked Robin.

'No,' they chorused.

'Apparently, he's staying in the village inn,' added Coral who always knew everything. 'The owner is a friend of his father's.'

'That doesn't surprise me, his father has friends everywhere,' said Godfrey with a little shrug. 'Fancy that idiot Thomas giving us such a fright!'

'What about you blowing that magic whistle!' taunted Romaric, ruffling Godfrey's hair.

'What about it! I couldn't know that we weren't in real danger!' said Godfrey defensively, smoothing his hair with the palms of his hands.

'I've got to hand it to you, you can sure keep a secret,' added Amber messing up his hair again.

'Stop it! Honestly, you can be such a pain!' he moaned, plastering his hair down again with his hands. 'Quadehar gave me the whistle at the beginning of the holidays so that I could warn him if Robin was ever in any danger! He asked me not to say anything to you. He entrusted it to me alone.'

'I bet he's kicking himself now!' teased Romaric.

'Oh, shut up! He did what he was supposed to do,' Robin interrupted. 'Thank you! Because if it had just been up to me to protect you ...'

'You can't say that,' Coral reassured him. 'Maybe if it had been a real Gommon, your magic powers would have come to the rescue again.'

'Maybe,' said Robin, unconvinced. 'OK guys, I have to go. See you later!'

'See you this evening!' they replied, watching him head off down the path that led to the glade where he met Master Quadehar under the big oak tree for his daily lesson.

Although it was only a couple of days since the incident with Thomas on the beach, it already felt like ages ago. The holidays weren't the same with Robin having to leave his friends for his lessons with the sorcerer. He spent the mornings and evenings with them, but the afternoons were devoted to studying magic. Today,

Romaric was going to spend his time training for the knighthood, and Godfrey wanted to practise scales on his zither. Only Amber and Coral were especially dissatisfied with this new arrangement, and were bored, having run out of tricks to play on the two boys. Luckily, during their evenings together they were allowed to stay up late into the night.

Robin soon reached the glade. Quadehar was sitting on the ground waiting for him, his eyes closed, leaning against the trunk of the oak. Robin cleared his throat to signal his presence.

'Come and sit by me,' said the sorcerer, who hadn't moved.

Robin joined him. As he sat beside his master, he carefully imitated his posture.

'Relax and absorb the energy of the tree which rises from its deepest roots to its topmost leaves. ...'

Robin closed his eyes and tried to concentrate. He felt nothing. ...

As if he able to read the boy's mind, Quadehar went on, 'It's a slow process. But don't worry, you don't need to overdo the concentration! Your spine will benefit all the same. Let's chat a little; you wanted to ask me something, yesterday?'

They had spent the previous afternoon reciting the twenty-four Graphems, over and over again, despite Robin's vain attempts to steer the conversation onto the subject of the incident on the cliffs.

'Yes, Master,' he replied enthusiastically, 'I wanted to know ...'

'Stay put with your back against the tree! Good, I'm listening.'

Robin adjusted his posture, then went on, 'How did you appear out of the rock, Master?'

The sorcerer laughed. 'Because I wasn't really inside it, my boy! I followed the paths of the Wyrd to reach you. First of all I worked out my route – in the same way that you plot your itinerary on a map with a compass – then, I entered the Wyrd by slipping inside an oak tree; I merely exited through a rock. That's all.'

'That's all?' exclaimed Robin, in astonishment. He could barely believe his ears. 'But how is that possible? You're in the forest, you knock on the door of a tree, it opens up, you run along a path, you open a window in a boulder and, hey presto, you're on a beach? That's just amazing!'

'It's not so amazing, Robin. It's just exhausting. It simply requires expertise in magic and a thorough knowledge of the Wyrd. I know – you tell me what you would have done.'

'Me?' protested the apprentice. 'What do you mean?'

'For example, how would you have got the tree and the rock to open and let you in and out of the Wyrd?'

'I ... I'd have ...'

'Think!' commanded Quadehar sternly. 'I'm waiting.'

'Er ... I'd have ... I'd have called Raidhu! The chariot, the Graphem of travel!'

'And then?' asked the sorcerer, whose face had lit up with encouragement. 'How would you have worked out the route and found your way through the Wyrd?'

'I'd have asked the help of Perthro, the Graphem that looks like a dice cup and is the guide in the Wyrd,' replied Robin with more assurance.

He felt the sorcerer's hand squeezing his shoulder affectionately.

'Well done, well done. You are beginning to understand many things. But it's all theoretical. It's much harder in practice, and much more dangerous. Recite the ancient poem of wisdom for apprentice sorcerers.'

Robin did so.

Know how to write and to interpret,
Feel the colours and the shapes
When to cast and when to cast off,
Then know your Graphem's measured fate.
Sometimes it's better not to ask the question
When the answer's in the Stars
Feel the strength as it grows within you
And find your gift will reap its own reward.

'One day, my boy,' Quadehar resumed, 'you will fully understand the meaning of those phrases. For the time being, remember that you must always remain humble and tread carefully when it comes to magic ... yes, you wanted to ask me something else?'

Robin was fidgeting as he always did when he was bursting to ask his master a question. 'Master Quadehar, what was that posture you took up against Thomas's shadow on the beach?'

'Now that's a good question! It was a Stadha, a

position that replicates the shape of a Graphem to increase its power had I needed to call it. ... In that instance, exhausted by my journey through the Wyrd, I adopted the stance of Naudhiz, the Graphem of Distress, which both neutralizes magic spells and resists physical attacks. Is there anything else you wish to know?'

'No, Master,' replied Robin thoughtfully, suddenly realizing what a long way he still had to go until he became a fully fledged sorcerer.

'Then let me be. I'm tired today. ... Practising magic takes its toll, just as going into battle leaves a knight exhausted! Off you go. See you tomorrow.'

Robin didn't have to be told twice, and he raced off back home.

He found his friends gathered in his room. They were thrilled to have him home earlier than expected. In celebration, they decided to organize a picnic out on the heath that evening and spend the night under the stars around a camp fire.

'Are you sure there's no risk of being attacked by Korrigans?' asked Coral for the fifth time. She was terrified. She'd heard so many stories about these wizened, dwarf-like creatures with cats' paws who were fond of playing pranks on humans.

'Absolutely none,' replied Romaric fastening his knapsack. 'Tell her, Godfrey, I'm sick of repeating myself.'

'At this time of year, lovely princess, the Korrigans only dance around menhirs and dolmen stones. So we simply need to choose a part of the heath where there aren't any. Anyway,' Godfrey added, 'tonight we'll be accompanied by a brave knight and a powerful sorcerer!'

'Ha, ha, ha ... very funny!' grinned Romaric. 'In the meantime, who's going to carry the rucksack with all the food in it? Not a wimp who'll get blown over by the first gust of wind!'

'Oh stop whingeing,' said Amber briskly. Then, she clapped her hands and imitated the authoritarian tones of a teacher, barking, 'Come along, my group, hurry up!'

Night fell slowly.

The friends had walked for ages before finding the ideal spot near an ash grove and surrounded by low rocks covered in lichen. They lit a fire, put the potatoes in the hot cinders, pricked the sausages and barbecued them on sticks over the embers. They had a feast, telling each other funny stories and laughing helplessly as they tucked into the food. Then they sang traditional songs of The Lost Isle which had been passed down through the generations. Romaric and Coral enthusiastically started a lively conversation about The Lost Isle in the days of yore, Romaric full of admiration for the bravery of the Knights of the Wind, and Coral envious of the finery worn by the ladies of the day depicted on ancient tapestries. Godfrey had taken his zither out of its case.

'This is so wonderful!' sighed Amber, lying on her back and listening to the melancholy sounds Godfrey drew from his instrument.

'It's a pity that life can't always be like this,' added Robin, who was lying next to her. With his hands clasped behind his head, he let his gaze roam among the stars.

Only their eyes could be seen shining in the dark. Yes, thought Robin, happy for once to be close to Amber, it's a pity that life isn't always like this!

15

Ambushed!

'What shall we do this afternoon?' brooded Coral.

The weather was gloomy and the friends, feeling the effects of too many late nights, were sprawled on the carpet in Robin's room. They'd already spent the morning lazing about, and could have quite happily stayed that way for the rest of the day.

'Oh come on,' urged Coral, suddenly restless. 'For once we've got Robin with us. Let's do something!'

Quadehar was away, having been summoned urgently to a monastery of the Guild, so his pupil was enjoying an unexpected afternoon of freedom.

'Let's go to the cinema,' suggested Godfrey.

'Good idea!' agreed Amber. 'What's on this week?'

'I think it's some old film about time-travel machines,' replied Coral. 'Right,' she went on, 'who's for the cinema?'

They all raised their hands, albeit rather half-heartedly.

'What flavour were you?' asked Godfrey, coming back from the refreshment kiosk.

'Vanilla, please!' said Amber

'I'm the same.'

'There, you see, we like the same things, Robin!' exclaimed Amber, loud enough for everyone to hear. 'It's a sign!'

Robin's green eyes shot daggers at her, while Godfrey and Romaric stifled a snigger. Since their night on the heath, Robin had thought that there was a sort of truce between Amber and him. For the last few days she hadn't been winding him up all the time, and it was very pleasant. But the ceasefire seemed to be over, and Robin sighed. Hadn't girls got anything better to do with their time than annoy boys? He fidgeted uncomfortably in his seat.

'Sssh!' said someone in the audience, 'the film's starting!'

The lights went down. For a while, Robin couldn't concentrate. He was unable to get Agatha's face and Amber's mocking smile out of his mind. He tried his best to forget them and absorb himself in the story. He had just about succeeded when he felt a hand trying to creep into his own. His heart leaped. It was Amber, next to him. Why did she want to hold his hand? Nobody could see them, so it couldn't be to embarrass him in front of the others. There must be another reason. Could it be, could it possibly be that she really liked him? His heart was racing. What should he do? Pretend he hadn't

noticed? Whisper to her to stop? He tried to stay cool.
Here he was, a would-be sorcerer, made to feel awkward
and unable to cope with holding hands with a girl! He
couldn't help blushing. He wanted to mumble something, but was scared that she'd make fun of him. What
on earth should he do? Luckily, by now, Amber had
given up and replaced her hand on the arm of her seat.
Robin quietly let out a sigh of relief.

'Do you think it's possible to travel back in time like they
did in the film?' Romaric asked his cousin.

When the show was over, they'd decided to take the
long way home through the forest, in order to make the
most of the fine weather that had greeted them when
they left the cinema. The sunlight dancing on the foliage
made pretty, dappled patterns.

'Yes, I think it's possible,' replied Robin. 'I don't know
how, but not with a machine!'

'It's really odd to think that in The Real World they
don't have magic!' remarked Romaric.

'There are even more amazing things,' replied Godfrey.
'For example, they don't have knights!'

'Can't you be serious for five minutes,' complained
Romaric. He went on in earnest, 'I don't know whether
you watch the news on TV, but they're in the process of
destroying their world.'

'Daddy always says,' said Amber who, like Robin, was
acting as though nothing had happened at the cinema,
'that the good thing about The Lost Isle is that it has kept
all the best things from The Real World.'

'Yeah, in any case, I don't envy them their polluted atmosphere and their water that stinks of chlorine,' continued Romaric. 'But I admit I'd love to ride in a car! A Porsche or a Ferrari!'

'And I'd like to swan up the steps at a Hollywood premiere!' added Coral, her eyes shining.

'What's that got to do with it?' retorted Romaric crossly.

'Oh, leave me alone!' replied Coral, peeved.

'Ssh!' said Robin, all of a sudden. 'Can you hear a strange noise?'

They froze. They were in the midst of the forest, and all around them they could hear the familiar sounds of nature – birds trilling, the breeze rustling the leaves, insects humming.

'No, I didn't hear anything,' replied Romaric.

'That's odd,' muttered Robin. 'I could have sworn I heard. ... Something's not right!'

He left the path and walked a few steps, scanning the clusters of trees. He was sure he'd heard some sort of growl, a dull, muffled growl like that of a bear. And yet there appeared to be nothing there. Not an animal in sight, not even a bush behind which something could be hiding. Nothing but trees too slender to conceal anything.

'Can you see something, Robin?' whispered Godfrey.

'No, I ...'

Suddenly, out of a pile of leaves, a colossal creature rose from the ground and stood before Robin. The friends shrieked in alarm and fear.

It was an Ork! One of those horrible monsters from The Uncertain World that The Shadow used in his armies.

Cousins of the Gommons, the Orks possessed the same massive build, power and cruelty, differing only in that they had adapted well to living on land, whereas the Gommons were more at home in the sea. They wore their stiff grey hair tightly pulled back and tied at the nape of the neck with a strip of oily cloth. In the middle of their coarse, wrinkled reptilian faces glinted two small beady eyes, while beneath their rough canvas and leather garments, their thick, cracked skin was like that of an elephant. Yet their exceptionally long legs made them very quick on their feet.

The Ork had been lying in wait for them beside the path, concealed in a pit covered with branches. It stood motionless in front of them, holding a club, its gaze shifting from one member of the petrified group to the other. So Robin *had* heard a growl!

'Whistle, whistle for goodness sake!' Romaric suddenly yelled at Godfrey, who had frantically yanked the whistle from his pocket and was blowing it as hard as he could.'

'I'm blowing! I'm blowing!'

Quadehar did not appear. As the realization that they were on their own hit the gang, a surge of panic rippled through them. They were about to run. But then a second Ork dropped nimbly down from the branches of a tree where it had been hiding, and blocked their escape.

Now, there were two, hunting together. Grunting

loudly, the first Ork brandished his club and lunged at Robin.

Robin took to his heels, and began weaving in and out of the trees, hoping to throw off the quick but ungainly creature. He could see that the second Ork was pursuing his friends, swinging his club. He had to think fast. They wouldn't be able to hold out for long! His master, clearly, was not coming to their rescue. And, again, even though they were in real danger, Thursaz was not acting of its own accord, spontaneously, as it had against the Gommon on the beach.

Instinctively, Robin ducked to avoid the huge, clawed hand that reached out to catch him by the hair. He pushed himself to run even faster.

'Amber!' screamed Coral. 'Amber!'

Like Robin, Coral was desperately trying to shake off the Ork that had started to chase her when they had scattered. Despite its bulk, it was carefully avoiding the branches that Coral threw in its path in a bid to slow it down. Looking over, Amber realized her sister was in danger and rushed to her aid.

'Take that, you monster!' she cried, throwing a huge fistful of earth at the Ork, blinding it momentarily and giving Coral a chance to get ahead.

The beast howled and turned its rage on the plucky girl. Romaric and Godfrey tried to entice the Ork towards them, shouting abuse and throwing sticks at it. But it was a waste of time. The furious creature was intent on attacking Amber, who, out of breath, was using every ounce of energy and cunning to duck the blows raining down on her.

Robin turned ashen. He had to help her! He was the only one who could do anything! Luckily, the Ork that had been chasing him was getting tired and Robin managed to put some distance between them. He changed course, heading in the direction of his friends. At the same time he tried to concentrate his mind, running through all the Graphems he could think of. When he got to Ingwaz, the twenty-second, the sign puffed itself up a little. Responding, he called it. At the same moment as he reached Amber, the two Orks drew level. The monsters exchanged a look and stopped in their tracks. As time stood still for a second, the five friends, anticipating the worst, gasped for breath.

Then, roaring and swinging their clubs above their heads with renewed fury, the two Orks, moving in unison, attacked the gang, scattering them screaming in all directions.

Only Robin didn't move. He closed his eyes. He needed to concentrate, to empty his mind, to forget these huge monsters that towered above him, armed with sharp teeth and terrifying weapons. Ingwaz shone in the darkness behind his closed eyelids. He took up the Stadha, the stance of the Graphem, opened his eyes and shouted, just as the Orks closed in on him, 'ING-WAAAAZ!'

The first Ork stopped dead, as if its feet were caught in the jaws of a trap. Rooted to the spot, it roared and flailed its arms helplessly. It couldn't move an inch! But its companion was still charging towards Robin.

Robin panicked. The Graphem for 'freezing' had only disarmed one of them! It was too late to invoke another. In any case, he knew he wouldn't have enough energy. The only solution was to run! Which was what he was about to do when suddenly a shape, emerging from the nearby trees, hit the Ork over the head, just as it made a lunge for Robin.

'Thomas!'

It was indeed Thomas who had miraculously jumped into the fray and was now fighting the monster for all he was worth! Gathering his wits, Robin grabbed a branch and joined in, careful to avoid injuring Thomas. Romaric, Amber and Godfrey ran to assist him. However, Thomas was no match for the monster – he was already losing blood and growing weaker from a bite on his arm. Furiously, the Ork – which had stumbled with this new onslaught – got to its feet, growling. Grabbing its young adversary by the throat, it lifted Thomas right off the ground. Then just at that moment, Quadehar appeared, racing along the path fighting for breath.

At the sight of the sorcerer, the monster froze. It let out a howl of terror, dropped Thomas and turned to run away. The sorcerer immediately called on the power of Ingwaz, and the Ork stopped in its tracks beside its companion, clawing helplessly in the dirt.

Quadehar hastened over to Thomas, who lay motionless on the ground.

16

The monastery of Gifdu

The huge grey horse borrowed by Quadehar from Uncle Urian carefully picked its way along the narrow path that wound through the Gifdu gorge. Robin, riding pillion behind the sorcerer, surveyed the dramatic landscape. They had left Penmarch at dawn, and now it was nearly dusk. He decided to break the silence that had fallen on them since they had remounted after eating lunch at a roadside inn.

'Master, do you think Thomas will be all right?'

'Don't fret, Robin. The Ork gave him a nasty bite, but he's over the worst now. Thank goodness I got there in time ...'

'It's unbelievable, Master, that someone could have stopped you entering the Wyrd to get to us.'

'Not someone, my boy – The Shadow! He seems to have increased his powers considerably and was able to prevent me entering the Wyrd for a good ten minutes! That is why we are going to Gifdu, Robin, to give our

Chief Sorcerer a detailed account of the latest events.'

'Lucky you were close to Penmarch when you heard the whistle!'

'More to the point, Robin, it's lucky I'm a fast runner!' They turned off onto an even narrower and steeper path.

Robin thought about the need for a sorcerer to be in good physical shape. At first, he was quite proud of having outrun the Ork in the forest. Then he realized that the effort had exhausted him, so when he wanted to call a second Graphem, he didn't have the energy to do so, nor did he have the strength to run away again. No, it was to Thomas and to him alone that he owed his life. The minute he got back, he'd have a word with his cousin Romaric about the two of them training together.

'By the way, congratulations on your 'freezing' spell, my boy,' Quadehar went on. 'What made you think of that?'

'It sort of came to me all by itself, Master. Not in the same way that Thursaz just came into my head on the beach against the Gommon, but instead it sort of suggested itself to me. But why didn't Ingwaz work against the second Ork?'

'Ingwaz is a selective Graphem that only works on one person. You needed to invoke it twice to stop both your attackers.'

Robin promised himself he'd become fitter. If only he'd had more energy, Thomas wouldn't have had to risk his life.

The horse's hooves sent showers of little stones flying up.

'May I ask you something, Master?'

'Isn't that what you've been doing anyway?'

'Er ... yes! But, may I, Master?'

'Yes do, Robin,' Quadehar encouraged him.

'On the beach, the first time, with Agatha and Thomas ... Agatha told me that apprentices couldn't cast spells. ... How come I managed to?'

There was a long silence.

The sorcerer finally replied, rather brusquely, 'Because you are especially gifted, Robin.'

They were coming up to a very difficult section of the path. Quadehar had to dismount to lead the horse. When the sorcerer had returned to the saddle, Robin questioned him again. 'Master? ...'

'Yes, my boy?'

'Why were the Orks afraid of you?'

Quadehar laughed softly. 'Because I've been to The Uncertain World so often that I'm becoming quite well known there. Well known and ... feared.'

'Master, do we have the same powers in The Uncertain World as we do here?'

'Yes and no, Robin. The power of the Graphems remains unchanged, but they behave differently. I can't explain that any more clearly for the moment. You have to experience it for yourself. ... To keep things simple, remember that we sorcerers effectively retain and sometimes even increase our powers in The Uncertain World.'

Robin couldn't think of anything else to say. They continued in silence until they reached the monastery of Gifdu, the jewel of the Guild, and headquarters to the supreme sorcerers' authority of The Lost Isle.

The monastery stood on a hilltop in the depths of the Gifdu gorge, which widened at this point before petering out as it reached the sheer Sorcerers' Mountain. The thick, grey walls blended into their surroundings so that they were almost indistinguishable from the rock face, apart from row upon row of symmetrical windows.

Because of the wind that blew continually in the gorge, the roof was neither thatched nor tiled, but was made of broad, flat stones that made the monastery appear to melt into the bleak landscape.

It was the first time that Robin had seen the monastery other than in books, and it took his breath away. The entire village of Penmarch would fit into this imposing building!

Quadehar noticed his pupil's look of surprise. 'Well, Robin? What do you think of Gifdu?'

'It's enormous, Master!' exclaimed the boy. 'How many sorcerers live here?'

'Oh, very few. About fifteen, maybe. But that's not its primary function. Most of the monastery is made up of libraries and study rooms. The main job of the sorcerers who live here is to look after them. The rest of the buildings house dormitories and dining rooms for members of the Guild who come here to study.'

'So they don't teach magic here?' asked Robin, sounding slightly disappointed.

'Magic isn't taught anywhere specific, Robin – it's taught everywhere! You just need a master and an apprentice. But later, when you want to find answers to your questions, then this is where you can come to seek them. ...'

'Was it from Gifdu, Master, that Yorwan stole the *Book of the Stars*?'

Quadehar's face clouded over. 'Yes, it was. But I should warn you that it's best not to mention the subject in the monastery. He left unpleasant memories behind him.'

Robin bit his lip. 'I'm sorry, Master.'

'Why sorry? You weren't to know. But now you do.'

They dismounted and, leading the horse by the bridle, climbed up a wider path hewn out of the rock. They soon stood before the only visible entrance to the monastery: a massive studded oak door, reinforced with steel plates.

'Wow!' breathed Robin in awe. 'That door must be pretty solid!'

'Indeed!' replied Quadehar. 'But what makes it truly impregnable is the Galdr, the incantations, the combinations of Graphems inscribed on it. We'll talk about them some other time.'

The sorcerer rang the big bell hanging by the entrance.

A few minutes later, a short, tubby almost bald man wearing spectacles and a flowing dark cloak like Quadehar's, came and opened the door. On seeing the visitors, his face broadened into a big smile.

'Quadehar!'

'Good to see you again, Gerald. It's been a long time!'

The two men exchanged the sorcerers' embrace.

'Let me introduce Robin, my pupil. ...

'Delighted to meet you, if I may say so,' replied Gerald, winking and vigorously shaking the boy's hand.

'Robin,' went on Quadehar, 'this is Gerald.'

'Is he the porter?' asked Robin innocently, disappointed that the man with such a heavy responsibility wasn't a giant.

The two sorcerers laughed.

'There's no porter here, young apprentice,' explained Gerald. 'The door of Gifdu is sufficient!'

'Gerald is our computer wizard,' Quadehar informed him.

'And I hope I'll see you often in the computer room during your stay here,' said the little man. 'Most apprentices think the Graphems are more fun and tend to forget the magic of microprocessors!'

Leaving the horse with Gerald, who led it to the stables, they turned down a very long corridor. Behind them, the door swung closed unaided.

᧕

'The Chief Sorcerer can't see us before tomorrow. So let's wander around the monastery.'

Quadehar had just joined his pupil in the little room they had been given in the south wing, on the third floor. It was simple and clean – two beds, a table and two chairs. In one corner, a door opened into a little bathroom. And the one heavily shuttered window afforded a breathtaking view of the gorge.

They left the room and set off to explore the monastery's never-ending corridors.

'These are the kitchens. ... That's the history library. ...

This is a study room. ... Over there is Gerald's computer room. ...'

They went through doors, crossed rooms, wandered down endless passageways. The place was a mix of every style of architecture, from classical to modern day, although predominantly medieval with freestone walls, vaults and arches. This lent the whole building a sense of order, but also one of tranquillity. Robin's eyes and ears were alert to his surroundings, but there were so many places to see that it was too much to take in at once.

'This is the patio, the only part of the monastery where noisy conversations are allowed. ... Over there is the library of The Uncertain World, which contains all the information we have on the subject. ... Here's the gymnasium. ...'

'A gym, Master?'

'Of course! Have you already forgotten the importance of physical exercise?'

They continued their tour of the imposing monastery, Quadehar guiding Robin through the maze of corridors which all looked identical, and night fell before they had finished. So they returned to the kitchens, where the sorcerer ordered a hearty meal, which he carried to their room on a tray. They ate hungrily, while watching the awesome sight of dusk gradually gathering over the gorge.

'Tomorrow, you will continue your tour of Gifdu on your own. I've got a busy day ahead. And now, it's bedtime.'

'Good night, Master Quadehar. Sweet dreams!'

'You too, Robin, you too.'

17

Robin turns hacker

Robin was down in the dumps. He and Quadehar had been at the monastery of Gifdu for nearly two weeks. They had already met the Chief Sorcerer twice, and the boy had told the gaunt old man everything he knew. He didn't understand why his master was extending their stay. The Gommon captured on the beach still hadn't talked. But what did that have to do with him? He was desperately missing Romaric, Godfrey, Amber and Coral. He felt as if he was betraying them somehow by staying away so long. And, above all, he was missing out on all the fun! Amber's face kept popping up in his mind, and he realized he was even missing being teased by the most annoying girl on The Lost Isle! That was a sure sign that the isolation was really beginning to get to him.

Quadehar left him alone most of the time. On the first day, he had given him permission – in a strangely amused tone – to roam the buildings. So Robin had set out to explore the monastery. Of course, like all the apprentices who came to Gifdu for the first time, in the beginning he had got lost and had to stand in the corridor calling out for ages before a sorcerer came to find him and show him the way back to his room. ...

To everyone's astonishment, Robin, set a challenge by his master, had discovered in a day what most novices took a week to find out. At certain points in the walls, carved stones (which the sorcerers of Gifdu called Talking Stones) gave directions! It had only taken him a further day to work out the signs engraved on them. And so he had thrown himself into exploring the monastery, and soon began to know his way around.

As there were no other apprentices at Gifdu with whom he could share the fun of discovery, Robin soon became a regular visitor to the monastery's many study rooms. That way, he made friends with several sorcerers. In addition to Gerald, whose dry humour appealed to him, there was Khadwan, who was in charge of the gymnasium. He was a solitary old man, astonishingly supple and strong for his age, whom Robin had impressed by telling him about his grim encounter with the Orks.

Every morning, he helped Eugene in the monastery's post room to sort the sacks of mail that arrived at Gifdu from all four corners of The Lost Isle. Humble citizens, clan chiefs, sometimes even Korrigans (Robin recognized their tiny, elaborate handwriting), all wrote asking the Guild to advise them or resolve their disputes.

Meanwhile, the sorcerers of Gifdu became fond of Robin, laughing at his antics and impressed at how seriously he took his role as apprentice sorcerer, wandering

between library and study room with his bag and notebook.

Robin learned a lot. But this situation was really
beginning to get him down. It looked like he was going
to end up spending his entire summer holiday here, far
from Penmarch and his friends. Surely he could always
come back to Gifdu later, in October or November, for
the Samain holidays?

His mind full of this problem, he stopped with a sigh
in front of a Talking Stone which suggested three different destinations. He set off down a dimly lit corridor in
the direction of the computer room.

After saying hello to Gerald who seemed absorbed in
sorting out a pile of disks, he sat down at a free terminal.
At this time of day – when everyone was having their
afternoon nap – there was not much activity at Gifdu,
especially as, over the last few days, the weather had
been suffocatingly hot and the computer room wasn't
exactly the coolest place to be. Robin put his bag down
on the table and switched on the computer.

He wasn't a computer whizz but, like most of The Lost
Isle students, he was sufficiently skilled to play computer games. He scrolled through the menu looking for a
game. Unable to find anything interesting, he launched
an advanced search to see if the computer contained
games that Gerald might have barred to stop the apprentices getting into them. When the search engine asked
him for the keyword, he typed in the word 'game'. The
reply came back at once, 'Not found'. Obviously, that
would have been too easy. He typed in 'entertainment',

but with no more success. Then he tried other synonyms, then the names of his favourite games. Nothing. He was about to give up after keying in 'The Master of the Keep', the game he loved best, when the search engine led him to an intriguing home page, with a background of a star-studded sky, that simply said, in beautiful copperplate handwriting, 'Password'.

'This is beginning to get interesting,' muttered Robin.

Then came twelve identical symbols each representing a letter or a number – a password so long that it would have taken Robin a lifetime to discover it.

He thought it odd that it should be so hard to get into a simple game. He was frustrated, but that only increased his determination. 'OK, we're on, mystery game!'

He bashed away at the keyboard to try and override the password, but it was impossible. His computer knowledge was too limited to hack into the system. He racked his brains. Suddenly, he had an idea. He feverishly opened a graphics program. Using the mouse, he painstakingly drew an image he'd copied time and time again for his master – Elhaz, the Swan Graphem that solved conundrums and unlocked doors!

Then he imported the drawing onto the home page with the starry sky and placed it in the password box. He waited. Nothing happened.

'Something must be missing,' muttered Robin, his mind racing.

Suddenly inspired, he plugged in the microphone and turned on the sound. Then he pressed his lips to it and murmured, 'By the might of the Ancestor and of the Rainbow, you who crackle when you burn – Elhaz. ...'

The Graphem on the screen began to glow, then seemed to dissolve, eating up the symbols of the password. The home page quivered then disappeared, revealing a new menu.

'Yessss!'

Robin punched the air. What game was this? He scanned the menu: 'Monastery accounts', 'Members of the Guild', 'Friends and enemies of the Guild', 'Current projects'. ... The list was long. He couldn't believe it, he had hacked into the central system! He certainly shouldn't be looking at this. He glanced over at Gerald, but the computer wizard was still classifying his disks.

'Calm down, calm down. Your intentions aren't evil. You're not trying to harm the Guild. So what you're doing isn't so bad. Just exit the program, switch off your computer and leave quietly. ...'

But while he was trying to talk himself into doing the right thing, Robin couldn't take his eyes off the lists of files with intriguing names that tempted his curiosity.

'*Plan of Gifdu*. Surely it's not a crime to have a quick look at that.'

He clicked on the icon and the monastery appeared in 3-D. Moving the cursor onto the places that interested him produced an enlarged image of the area with explanatory notes. To think he believed he'd seen the whole place! There was as much of Gifdu underground as there was above ground.

Robin wished he could go everywhere. But afternoon

nap was over and a few sorcerers were already beginning to wander into the room. He felt it was wiser to stop there.

He clicked on 'print' to print out the plan of the monastery, hesitated and finally decided to print out the directory list of all the files in the program too. Then he carefully shut down all the screens he'd opened and switched off the computer. He stuffed the printouts into his bag and left the room, calling goodbye to the plump Gerald who was still busy, and merely raised his hand.

18

The price of curiosity

Several more days passed. This morning, Robin stayed in bed later than usual. Sometimes he liked to lie in bed and daydream. In one fantasy, he pictured Amber and himself, on the heath, by the campfire – she apologized to him for all the times she'd been horrid to him! He generously forgave her and, after fighting off a horde of Orks, even gave her a hug to show her he wasn't angry! Daydreaming was fun, but it was no more than a way of keeping boredom at bay, just as he had hacked into the central computer as a way of amusing himself, and forced himself to keep busy by going backwards and forwards between the gym, the libraries and his room.

But he was still missing Romaric, Godfrey, Coral and Amber.

What were they doing right now? He pictured them camping out under the stars without him. He sat bolt upright and leaped out of bed. He had to do something! Talk to Quadehar! The sorcerer had come to his rescue before to save his holiday when they had been to see the Provost. Surely he'd step in again! Robin grabbed his canvas bag and set off in search of his master.

He asked Gerald, who told him that Quadehar was in the Chief Sorcerer's tower, but was sorry he couldn't tell him the way, as apprentices weren't allowed there. Robin begged and pleaded but the computer wizard would not give in, so Robin took his leave. Suddenly, he had an idea. Looking around to make sure he was alone, he took out of his bag the plan of the monastery he'd printed off the computer. He hadn't yet taken the time to study it properly but he found he had no difficulty locating Charfalaq's office, thanks to some very clear directions. It was in the north tower, at the top of a very long, spiral staircase.

Robin decided to go there. He stole down the corridors as stealthily as a cat, pressing himself against the wall at the slightest sound.

As he climbed the stairs of the tower, Robin faltered. Wavering over whether or not he should be doing this, he could feel his resolve deserting him. Was it because he was afraid of approaching the Chief Sorcerer? Or was it a Galdr – a spell – holding him back? In his uncertainty, Robin softly invoked Naudhiz, to neutralize any curses, and then he called more vigorously on Isaz, the Ice Graphem which helped to reinforce the will. As Isaz glowed and shook him up inside, he felt his energy condense and harden. Then he continued up the stairs.

At last Robin reached the solid, studded door which led to the apartments of the Chief Sorcerer. It stood half open. He was just about to knock, when he heard the voices of the Chief Sorcerer and Quadehar coming from within. He decided to eavesdrop:

'... your apprentice's happiness does not count for much, my dear Quadehar. The boy will stay here as long as necessary. A month, a year if need be! I'll take full responsibility as far as the Provost is concerned.'

'Please consider the matter, Chief Sorcerer, I admit I slightly underestimated the danger, but ...'

'Slightly?' went on the hoarse voice. 'The boy came within a hair's breadth of being kidnapped and you dare say 'slightly'?' The Chief Sorcerer had a coughing fit. When it was over, he went on, 'No, there's no safer place for him to be than Gifdu. The subject is closed. For goodness sake, Quadehar, you know that The Shadow wants this boy, don't you? Do you want to hand him over on a plate?'

'No, no, of course not. That's why we took him under our wing at once. But do you really think that The Shadow will come looking for him here?'

'He wants him at all costs, that's a fact. The only thing that has saved him so far is the stupidity of the Gommons. The one we captured told us that they had been sent to The Lost Isle to capture a child wearing a sun pendant. I think that was the only instruction they'd managed to get into their thick skulls! Who knows how that girl came to have it in her possession? In any case, the mix-up has given us a respite, and the boy is our main weapon against The Shadow. If he stays here, The Shadow will have to come in person to capture him, for no Gommons or Orks would dare venture into Gifdu!'

'What you say makes sense,' sighed Quadehar. 'I just fear that Robin is not happy here. ...'

'Nevertheless, it's the best place for him. Here he has the biggest libraries in the land at his disposal. And the most knowledgeable people.'

'You don't remember what it's like to be a child, Chief Sorcerer. At that age, you don't think like an adult. I'm afraid it's fun and friendship they want, not books and teachers. And that is particularly true of Robin.'

'Absurd. There you are, worrying about your pupil, while we're trying to find out how The Shadow manages to send his monsters wherever he pleases, without bothering to use The Door!'

The voices were getting closer. Robin didn't dare hang around any longer. He turned around and fled down the stairs as silently as he could.

What did this all mean? So the Gommon had talked at last and the Guild hadn't even informed the Provost! The Lost Isle was in peril, The Shadow wanted to kidnap him for some unfathomable reason, and it turned out that it was his fault that Agatha was rotting away somewhere in The Uncertain World. What's more, he was being kept prisoner in the monastery – he'd heard it from Charfalaq's own lips! For his safety, or whatever – the fact was that he was being held captive. Robin almost cried in frustration. His master hadn't been able to do anything about it. He even felt guilty about that! Quadehar had been blamed because he'd allowed Robin his freedom in Penmarch, and this horrid old man had even dared scold him! This business was definitely going too far. The feeling that everybody around him had deceived him filled him with resentment. There were now two options. He could be a good boy and do what he was told and what was expected of him – or he could disobey and follow his intuition.

Robin walked past the Nature library without stopping. He bounded angrily four steps at a time up the stairs that led to the monastery's pigeon house. They were treating him as a prisoner, so then he'd behave like a prisoner!

He tiptoed silently across the vast square room that hummed with the beating of wings and the cooing of the hundreds of pigeons that were used to carry the Guild's secret correspondence up and down the country. Luckily, there was nobody there.

One day, when he'd been helping Eugene sort the post, the sorcerer had explained to him how the pigeon post worked.

Now, Robin walked over to the sorcerer's desk, scribbled a hasty message on the special, flimsy paper and slid it into a little metal tube which he sealed with blue wax. He picked up a label on which he wrote: *Romaric Penmarch, c/o Alicia Penmarch.*

Keeping his eye on the corridor, he caught the bird sitting in the pigeonhole labelled Penmarch, stroked it and tied the tube and label to its leg. Then he went over to the window and threw the pigeon up into the air. Miles away, in the Penmarch pigeon house, someone would receive the message bearing the confidential seal of the Guild and would go, without asking any questions, and deliver it by hand to his cousin.

The bird spread its wings and very soon was just a tiny dot in the sky.

19

The escape

It was several days since Robin had sent his carrier pigeon off on its journey. Nobody seemed to have noticed, and life for him at Gifdu went on as usual. Quadehar still hadn't seen fit to inform his pupil of the Chief Sorcerer's decision concerning his fate. Either he had business to attend to, or, perhaps simply to avoid Robin, he disappeared for the whole day and only returned to the little room late at night. Meanwhile, Robin busied himself investigating the various libraries, looking for secret information which he copied down into his notebook like a spy on a mission. He also spent a lot of time in the gym and Kadwa taught him 'Greeting the Day', a series of daily exercises to be done in the morning on waking. He also showed him the basic movements of Quwatin, the ancient martial art of The Lost Isle.

Some other apprentices had arrived at the monastery, accompanying their masters, but Robin was content to

keep his distance. He didn't care if they took his aloof-
ness for arrogance. He just didn't feel like making new
friends. His old friends seemed to have forgotten him
and his conviction that they would respond to his pigeon
message, which had so clearly told them how to find
him, had faded. He even wondered how he could have
imagined that his friends would abandon their pleasant,
carefree life in Penmarch and come all the way to Gifdu
to help him in his crazy enterprise!

The thought that Romaric and the others had just left
him to his sorry fate made him spiteful, and he took out
his frustration on the novices by making a false Talking
Stone out of paper maché, which confused them completely and sent them off to the laundry room in the
basement! After all, why should he be the only one to
have his holiday ruined? His trick got him into hot water
with the Bursar of Gifdu, a tall, bearded sorcerer with a
stern expression, but his only punishment was to be
deprived of dessert for a day, and Gerald managed to slip
him one anyway!

That morning, Robin lay in bed stretching lazily. A
glance to his right informed him that Quadehar had
already left. He sighed; another day far from Penmarch.
... He got up and went into the bathroom.

He was drying himself with his towel when he heard a
dull thud in the room – like the sound of a stone landing
on the floor. He rushed over to the bathroom window
and there, at the foot of the monastery wall, were
Romaric, Godfrey, Amber and Coral trying to hide themselves among the rocks! They were throwing stones at his

bedroom window, which had been left open and from which he had hung a red handkerchief, just as in his message.

How silly he'd been to doubt them! Of course they had answered his call for help! How could he have imagined that his friends wouldn't come? After all, wouldn't he have moved mountains for any one of them? He was so mad with himself for questioning their loyalty.

Another pebble landed on the floor.

He hastily pulled on his clothes, grabbed his apprentice's bag and a huge rucksack which he put on his back. From under his mattress he fished out a rope which he'd stolen from a cupboard in the gym, and tied it firmly to the hook for fastening the shutters. He ran the other end down his back and tied it around his thigh. Then he straddled the window, watched anxiously by the gang of friends. He inched his way down as best he could in a sitting position, his feet flat against the high wall. Several times, Amber, Coral, Godfrey and Romaric had to stop themselves from shouting encouragement. They had to be careful not to draw unwanted attention to Robin's escape.

Robin was making his way with difficulty. Great gusts of wind kept forcing him to spread his legs wide in order to keep his balance. Luckily the stone wall was dry and smooth, and his feet were able to get a good grip. He did, however, make the mistake of looking down, which made him giddy, and he had to pause for a while to steady himself. His eyes shut, his courage returned and he managed to control his trembling muscles and continue his long descent. Seen from below, Gifdu was forbidding, but from this vantage point it was all the more awe-inspiring! The chafing of the rope burned his hands. He gritted his teeth and continued and at last his feet touched solid ground, much to the relief of his friends below.

Even though his legs were still shaking, Robin raced over to the group. After a tearful reunion, Robin knew they must all get under cover. It was dangerous to stay out in the open like this.

'Come on, we mustn't hang around!' he urged.

The friends ran towards the gorge, stopping to catch their breath behind a big rock, out of sight of the monastery.

'Whew!' panted Robin. 'I never thought I'd make it. ... What a nightmare!'

'It was a nightmare getting here!' protested Godfrey.

'Yes, it really is the middle of nowhere,' added Coral.

'So you got my message, then?' inquired Robin who was gradually getting his breath back.

'Of course we did,' grunted Romaric. 'We wouldn't be here if we hadn't!'

'We couldn't believe it when the master of the pigeon house walked up to Romaric and gave him a message from the Guild!' exclaimed Coral. 'At first we thought you'd been kidnapped.'

'I had, in a way,' said Robin wryly.

'And then, when we read the message,' went on Coral. '*Held captive in the Monastery of Gifdu. Come and get me out of here. I'll put a red handkerchief outside my bedroom window. Remember to bring food. ...*'

'Did you remember?' asked Robin.

'Don't worry,' Amber reassured him. 'We hid our things in the gorge. Sorry we took so long, but we had to think up a story to tell your mother and to make preparations.'

'Then we had to find the wretched monastery,' Godfrey broke in. 'Those sorcerers are really twisted, going off to live in a place like this.'

'So what about Gifdu,' said Coral, her eyes bright with curiosity. 'It's one of the most secret places in the whole of The Lost Isle. Tell us about it!'

'Hold it, hold it ... you're forgetting that, even though I've run away, I'm still sworn to secrecy by the apprentice's vow. Anyway, we'd better not hang around here: Quadehar won't realize I've gone until this evening, but we need a head start.'

'Can you at least tell us where we're going?' moaned Romaric.

'You'll soon find out. Let's go!'

The five friends began to pick their way carefully along the narrow path through the Gifdu gorge.

ᕀ

They arrived in Dashtikazar as dusk was falling. When they emerged from the gorge, a kind man gave them a lift in his ramshackle cart, and another dropped them off just outside the capital. During the summer, nobody was surprised to see groups of young people on the road – after all, it was the school holidays.

'And now, where are we going?' demanded Romaric,

who was becoming increasingly irritated by Robin's refusal to share his plans.

'To The Doors to the Two Worlds,' announced the apprentice calmly.

They all froze.

'To ... to The Doors to the Two Worlds?' exclaimed Coral, astonished.

'Are you crazy?' asked Romaric staring at his cousin as if he were insane.

'Calm down, everyone!' said Godfrey. 'Suppose you tell us why?'

Robin paused for a moment, then nodded. 'All right. To tell you the truth, I want to pay a visit to The Uncertain World.'

'That's it,' groaned Romaric, 'I knew it. He's gone mad!'

'Listen,' explained Robin. 'I had time to do a lot of thinking in Gifdu. And I don't intend to spend the rest of my life shut up in a monastery, that's for sure! But I learned some terrible things there, things I'm not meant to know. About The Shadow, and about Agatha.'

'Agatha?' cried Godfrey. 'The kidnapping was terrible. But I thought there was no love lost between you two?'

'I know this might sound crazy,' went on Robin, 'but The Shadow is after me. It was me the Gommon wanted on the beach. Agatha was kidnapped instead of me. It's my fault she's a captive in The Uncertain World. I must try and save her! But I'm not asking you to understand, just to help me.'

'What do you want us to do?' asked Coral quietly.

'I want you to watch what I do very closely, so that if it goes wrong, you can go and tell Quadehar everything. And ask him to forgive me for disobeying him.'

'And how do you plan to get near The Doors, huh?' Romaric said discouragingly. 'It's impossible, there are knights guarding them all the time.'

'I have faith in my magic.'

'And how will you open them? You're just a little apprentice, not a great sorcerer. You're not even a junior sorcerer!'

'I have faith in my magic,' repeated Robin simply.

Amber, who had been silent so far, went up to Robin and looked him straight in the eye. 'You're not going anywhere alone, Robin. Either we come with you or we take you back to Gifdu bound hand and foot.'

'Don't be daft!' grinned Robin.

'No, she's right,' said Romaric who still wasn't quite sure how to take all this, but had no intention of missing out on a bit of action. 'Right, Godfrey? Coral?'

'We're with you,' assented Godfrey. 'You've deserted your friends for long enough as it is.'

'Are you sure there's no danger?' fretted Coral.

'Have you forgotten, princess? We're travelling with a fierce knight and a powerful sorcerer,' smiled Amber.

They laughed at Coral's crestfallen expression, then they formed a circle, placing their hands over each other's, and swore, like the Three Musketeers, 'All for one and one for all!'

'I don't know how to thank you for this. What you're doing is wonderful,' said Robin, deeply moved.

'Bah!' shrugged Romaric, winking at him. 'That's what friends are for, right?'

'Even so,' replied Robin, 'it was amazing enough that you came all the way to Gifdu to get me. You don't have to do anything else.'

'Personally,' teased Amber, 'I'm curious to see you running to the rescue of that stuck-up Agatha Balangru! In fact, I wouldn't miss it for the world!'

They left the city behind them and set off for the hill where The Doors to the Two Worlds stood.

20

The Doors to the Other Worlds

The Doors to the Two Worlds really did look like doors. They were very high and wide, and made of oak. Covered with hundreds of carved Graphems, they looked exactly like the entrance to the Monastery of Gifdu, except they were so old that nobody knew when they had been built, and they didn't lead into any building.

There was absolutely nothing on either side of The Doors. They stood alone, on a bare hilltop, guarded from below by the encampment of the Knights of the Wind. Ordinarily, there were two sentries guarding the place. But, because of The Shadow's recent incursions into The Lost Isle, there were now ten knights keeping watch.

'Our troubles begin!' hissed Godfrey, as he and his friends hid behind a large rock. 'Now what do we do, Robin?'

'What we'd planned,' replied Robin, calmly. 'We just have to wait until they're all together.'

'You're not going to kill them are you?' asked Coral worriedly.

'Yes, that's right,' said Romaric sarcastically, 'he's going to let out a great yell, fall on them and strangle them one by one with his own bare hands!'

'Mind you,' went on Godfrey in the same tone, 'if he takes them by surprise ...'

'Don't be horrible,' said Coral, getting upset.

'Well, stop talking rubbish,' snapped her sister.

'Shut up, you two,' said Robin. 'You're making too much noise. No, of course I'm not going to kill them. I'm just going to put a spell on them.'

That silenced them all and they waited patiently, without moving.

Romaric was desperately curious to see what his cousin was going to do. 'Hey, Robin,' he asked, 'what'll happen once we get to where we're going, I mean, to The Uncertain World?'

'We'll carry out our mission, that's all.'

'Our mission? What mission?' asked Coral, frowning.

'You know – rescuing Agatha from the clutches of the super-evil Shadow, giving the nasty Gommons who kidnapped her a good hiding, and plucking the hairs from the nostrils of the beastly Orks who attacked us,' joked Amber with a grin.

'You're not funny,' answered Coral primly. 'I just wanted to know what the plan was.'

'The plan,' said Robin rummaging around in the

mysterious rucksack he'd brought from Gifdu, 'is, first of all, to disguise ourselves. Otherwise we won't get far before we have problems.'

He flung down a package of clothing wrapped in plant-based plastic (of the environmentally sound type used on The Lost Isle) and tore it open.

'These are brilliantly useful cloaks which are worth a lot where we're going,' Robin told his friends who were staring at him round-eyed. 'They're worn by the Little Men of Virdu, who are the bankers of The Uncertain World. Their city, Virdu, is very close to a mountain range that's full of precious stones. They began mining them a long time ago and now the stones are used as the currency there. Wait a minute, and I'll explain more.'

Robin fished around in his bag and pulled out a leather pouch and a map which he spread out in front of the other four.

'There,' he announced proudly running his finger over the paper. It was a map of The Uncertain World. It took me a whole afternoon to copy it without being seen, when I was at Gifdu. There's Virdu. We should arrive here, on one of the Middle Islands, where it says "The Door to the World". The rest, though, is as much a mystery to me as it is to you.'

Then he opened the leather pouch which contained around thirty sparkling precious stones. 'Here's our spending money for the trip, generously provided by the Guild! We're not that rich, which is why I took these cloaks, so we can sell them if necessary.'

'Did they really give you those precious stones?' asked

Godfrey in amazement, playing with a diamond.

'Er, not exactly,' said Robin awkwardly. 'Let's say it's a loan. We'll share them out, it'll be safer.'

Robin began to distribute them.

Then they turned their attention to the six cloaks lying on the ground.

'Why do we have to dress up as Little Men of Virdu?' asked Coral dubiously as she gazed at the long, flowing grey cloak.

'Why? First of all, because the people of The Uncertain World fear and distrust them, so they leave them alone – which suits us fine! Secondly, because they are small, like us. And lastly, because it's the only costume from The Uncertain World that I found in the Gifdu storehouse. ... Here, all of you, take a cloak.'

'And what language are we supposed to speak?' asked Amber putting hers on.

'Ska, of course, like everyone else there. I hope you didn't skip your Ska lessons.'

'No, we should be OK,' said Amber who seemed convinced by Robin's arguments. 'How come you know so much about The Uncertain World?'

'I had plenty of time at Gifdu to read nearly every book on the subject.'

'Fine, and what treats are in store for us right now?' asked Romaric who was fed up with hanging around.

'Maybe we could have a bite to eat,' suggested Coral.

'Good idea, little sis,' approved Amber. 'But we'd better ration ourselves. We only brought provisions for Robin and there are five of us.'

'Let's share out the food,' said Robin, putting the extra cloak away in his rucksack. 'Then, I advise you all to copy my map of The Uncertain World, in case I lose it. Besides, we've got time. We'll have to wait till evening for the knights to gather together.'

They ate sparingly while making careful copies of Robin's map, snug in their comfortable Little Men of Virdu cloaks.

Robin gazed at the sky as he munched. He thought about the dangerous adventure into which he was dragging his friends. Was it recklessness or daring? He didn't recognize himself. What did he have in common with the old Robin? He felt strong, very strong. A thought crept into his mind – perhaps the Graphems were gradually transforming him, without his realizing it? Perhaps he could become a brave sorcerer, after all.

A movement beside him broke his thoughts.

'Hey, cousin Robin,' whispered Romaric in his ear, 'now, tell me the truth.'

'Tell you the truth?' replied the puzzled Robin also in a whisper, 'what do you want me to tell you?'

'I don't know ... that you're on a secret mission for the Guild, or the Provost, or whoever! But tell me that you know something that we don't!'

'Honestly, Romaric, I don't understand. I'm not on a mission for anybody! Not for the Guild or for the Provost! I told you everything before – visiting The Uncertain World is my idea and mine alone.'

'So my cousin really is stark raving mad,' groaned Romaric who realized that Robin wasn't kidding. 'But if what you say is true, we've had it.'

'What's up with you?' asked Godfrey drawing closer, followed by the two girls. 'Don't make so much noise, or the knights will hear us.'

'We're doomed!' spluttered Romaric. 'Can't you see? Hel-lo! Get real! We're five kids, led by a scrawny little guy who fancies himself as a sorcerer and wants to drag us off to the most evil world in the universe. ...'

'A fine way for a would-be knight to behave, blubbering like a girl,' taunted Amber, glaring at him.

'Stop it, all of you, please!' begged Robin. 'Let's get this clear once and for all: I'm not forcing you to come with me. You can still change your minds. But I've started something and I'm going to see it through to the end.'

'Bravo!' applauded Amber, clapping Robin on the shoulder, like Urian Penmarch. 'Spoken like a man!'

'Control yourself, sister,' chipped in Coral, 'that's a powerful sorcerer you're thumping.'

'All of you are bonkers,' sighed Romaric.

'All the same, Robin,' said Godfrey, 'you have to admit that we are setting off into the unknown.'

'Hang on a minute,' said Coral. 'We haven't left yet! Robin's got to open The Door first.'

'No problem,' replied Robin, rubbing his shoulder. 'I'm certain of the magic words.'

'Have you already tried them out?' asked Coral.

'No, but they're perfectly clear in my mind.'

'In his mind. ... Oh, then everything's fine, we're saved,' sighed Romaric, so theatrically that they couldn't help laughing.

Coral still wasn't convinced. 'But Robin,' she said, 'supposing we do get to The Uncertain World, how will we get back again?'

'If I can get us there,' replied Robin, 'I can get us back again. Have faith.'

21

The Doors

Later, at nightfall, the knights gathered by their tents for the evening meal. This seemed like the right opportunity to act, and Robin stood up. He checked that the wind was still blowing in the direction of the camp, then closed his eyes and concentrated. He called upon Dagaz, the Graphem in the form of an hourglass that could distort time or even make it stand still when it was used correctly.

Robin had learned from his master, at Gifdu, during one of the rare moments they had spent together, that not all the Graphems were invoked by yelling, and that often the same Graphem had different functions, depending on whether its name was shouted or whispered.

When he could see Dagaz clearly, Robin whispered it into the wind, which carried it to the knights' camp:

'Daaaagaaz ...'

The effect was not instant, but it was certainly spectacular. The knights carried on with their activities for a minute, seeing to the fire, cleaning their weapons or stirring the gruel in the cooking pot. Then, their movements gradually slowed down, as if those sturdy warriors in armour had been overcome by numbness. But nothing in their expressions betrayed the slightest panic. It was as though they were completely unaware of what was happening to them.

Finally, they appeared to stop in mid-movement, like the citizens of Pompeii, petrified for ever under the hot ash from the volcanic eruption as they went about their day-to-day activities.

Robin's friends cried out in astonishment. This wasn't the first time they'd seen Robin doing magic. They'd already seen him freeze an Ork to the spot in the forest of Penmarch. But this spell was much more impressive.

'Wow!' said Romaric open-mouthed.

'Awesome. ...' was all Godfrey could say.

Amber too was clearly impressed. Fascinated, she stared at Robin. He tried to look cool. He may have made remarkable progress in the art of magic, but he still couldn't help blushing to the roots of his hair at his friends' open-mouthed admiration.

'Have you turned them into statues?' asked Coral who couldn't take her eyes off the static forms down below.

'No. ... They're still moving, but so slowly they look as if they're frozen! At the moment time is moving more slowly for them than it is for us. That way we can walk past them without them seeing us. We'll be moving much too fast for their eyes. ...'

'Well, my friend,' whistled Romaric, 'I have to tell you that I'm seriously impressed.'

'Yes, er ... thank you ... right, let's not waste any time, it's getting dark.'

They ran through the knights' camp, shuddering at the vacant gaze of the motionless men. Coral stopped for a second to stare closely at a captain with a bushy beard who had been sharpening his sword. Romaric pulled her by the arm.

'Wait a minute! But ... it's true – they are moving!' exclaimed Coral. Look, Romaric, if I put this little pebble on the sword just here, right by the whetstone, he'll knock it off. ... There, you see?'

'Yes, I see, I see,' granted Romaric who felt uncomfortable surrounded by all these proud warriors neutralized in the space of a few minutes by a puny little apprentice sorcerer. 'Come on, let's hurry up and join the others. They're already at The Doors!'

Coral, who didn't want to stay behind on her own, reluctantly left her experiments. They ran over to their friends.

'Which one is it?' asked Godfrey trying to read the signs carved into the wood.

'This one,' replied Robin without hesitation, pointing to the door on the right, having glanced at the Graphems inscribed on it.

'Are you sure?' asked Coral. 'Because I don't want to end up in The Real World!'

'Why not? You could go to Hollywood and meet all the stars, after all,' Godfrey teased her.

'Stupid!' she replied, giving him a push.

'Sssh!' said Robin irritated. 'I have to cast a spell to open The Door and it's my first time, remember. I need silence so I can concentrate.'

'It's true, it's his first time,' fretted Coral. 'And you're certain that ...'

'I'm certain of my spell, but not of the outcome.'

'But you were saying, not even an hour ago ...' she protested.

'... that I would open The Door, and that is what I'm going to do. After that, I don't know what will happen. That's why I would have liked a witness who would be able, if things go wrong, to go and explain everything to Master Quadehar. In the hope that he'd be prepared to come to our rescue.'

'A witness,' Amber thought fast, 'any witness?'

'Yes, anybody who's not too stupid.'

'Well, I don't know if he'll be any good,' sighed Amber, 'but there's always that idiot whose been following us for a while and is about as subtle as a herd of elephants. Thomas! Come out of your hole and get over here!'

To everyone's surprise, Thomas Kandarisar emerged from behind a bush and his bulky form came lumbering towards them.

'I don't believe it!' said Romaric angrily. 'Hey, how long have you been spying on us?'

'Oh, drop it,' said Amber. 'In any case, I'm the only one who noticed he was following us, so what difference does it make? Besides, now we need him, for real. ...'

'Amber's right,' broke in Robin. 'Be quiet!'

He spoke to Thomas, whose arm was still heavily bandaged and in a sling as a result of his battle with the Ork.

'Thomas, do you think you can memorize everything I'm about to do to get to The Uncertain World?'

Thomas, completely indifferent to the reactions of the rest of the gang until now, nodded. He gazed devotedly at Robin.

'If it looks to you as if things have gone wrong, go straight to Master Quadehar and tell him everything. If it looks as though everything's gone well, wait for seven days. If you don't hear from us within a week, go and see him and explain. But not before. And I want you to go straight back to my mother now, and tell her we're on an important mission, and to trust me. Is that clear?'

Thomas muttered his reluctance to leave Robin, but nodded again to show he'd understood. He fumbled in his pockets and took out a strange object that appeared to be made of silver. On it there was a picture of a lion surrounded by flames.

'Here, Robin,' he said, stepping forward and holding out the medallion to the apprentice sorcerer. 'This is for you. I took it from the Ork I fought the other day. It might come in useful.'

They huddled over the object and examined it carefully. It was their only real clue about where to look for Agatha in The Uncertain World.

'Thank you, Thomas,' replied Robin gravely, slipping the medallion into his bag and walking towards The Doors. 'Oh! One last thing, don't hang around here for too long. The spell I put on the knights will wear off in one hour ... are the rest of you ready?'

Romaric, Godfrey, Amber and Coral moved closer to Robin who stood before The Door to The Uncertain World.

'Hold each other's hands and don't let go – whatever happens.'

In his left hand, Robin grabbed the hand being held out to him by Amber. Then he concentrated. Reciting a Galdr – a spell – was more complicated than invoking a Graphem.

First of all he called Raidhu, the Chariot, the Graphem of travel, then he invoked Eihwaz, the Ancient Tree – this would establish communication between the different worlds. All seemed to be going according to plan. Then the two Graphems had to be called at the same time and woven together, which took a long time. His companions, who, despite feeling despondent and beginning to grow impatient, were afraid to move, or even speak, and hardly dared breathe. At last, in a nervous voice, touching the signs on The Door to The Uncertain World with his right hand, Robin murmured the incantation:

'By the power of the Way, of Nerthus, Ullr and of The Double Branch, Raidhu below and Eihwaz in front, take us! RE! ...'

There was the sound of a door creaking. The friends each squeezed the hand they were holding a little tighter. To their amazement, they saw the stars disappear. A powerful draught sucked them through The Door and they were hurled into a black hole, then caught in a terrifying whirlwind.

In front of Thomas's astonished eyes, The Door to The Uncertain World lit up – and Robin, Romaric, Godfrey, Amber and Coral vanished in a flash.

22

The Moving Hills

It seemed to Robin that only a second had passed. In the time it had taken just to close his eyes and open them again, the place they had been in a moment ago had given way to strange grassy hills stretching as far as the eye could see, their silhouettes making humped shapes in the dark. Night had fallen, and a slender crescent moon shone amid the stars. Behind him, a single door stood outlined in the hollow of a little valley, a door similar to the one they had just stood before on The Lost Isle. There was nothing else in sight. Nothing, and nobody. Nobody. ...

Robin suddenly felt terribly afraid. The others. Where were the others?

He ran frantically to and fro, and shouted himself hoarse, in vain. Eventually, he sank breathlessly onto the grass and put his head in his hands. What could have happened? Where could Romaric, Godfrey, Amber and Coral be? They couldn't have vanished, they had all been holding hands a few minutes earlier. What about all his master's words of wisdom: 'Caution and humility, the sorcerer's watchwords. ...' Had he been cautious? No. Or humble? Certainly not. He had been arrogant. He, the so-called gifted sorcerer's apprentice, who nothing and nobody could resist, had believed that the door would obey him! Oh, what had he done?

He gradually calmed down and began to think. He had to be logical. How could the Galdr have gone wrong? It had opened The Door, he had ended up in The Uncertain World, but he was alone. All alone. Robin froze. Suddenly, he realized. How could he have forgotten to include Wunjo the Standard, the Graphem whose chief function was to bind together individuals with the same aim? He shouldn't have called *RE* but *WRE*! He mentally recited the Galdr as he should have said it: *By the power of the Generous and the Way, of Nerthus, Ullr and the Double Branch, Wunjo above, Raidhu below and Eihwaz in front, lead us! WRE!*

He was furious with himself for his mistake, but at the same time couldn't help feeling relieved too. The Graphem he'd forgotten merely kept the group together, which at least meant his friends hadn't been trapped in the whirlwind somewhere between the two worlds. They had no doubt landed in The Uncertain World too, only all in different places. But where? He took the map out of his bag and peered at it in the pale moonlight. He gazed about him. He hadn't arrived through the 'official' door, which was on an island, for the place he was in clearly bore no resemblance to an island. Everything suggested that he must be here on the map, somewhere called the Moving Hills. The best thing to do, when it was daylight, would probably be to get to the nearest town, and that was ... yes, Ferghana, which looked about a day or two's walk away. Although he desperately wanted to find his friends, he knew he needed to sleep to gain some energy for the task that lay ahead. Robin lay down on the grass, wrapped in his comfortable Virdu cloak. At least it had been a good idea to divide up his gear and share his knowledge of The Uncertain World with his friends. A secret hope grew inside him. They all had a map, and they had all seen the picture on the medallion that Thomas had given him. Surely, the logical thing would be for Godfrey, Romaric and the two sisters to follow that clue. In any case, that was what *he* intended to do. And, he told himself, if the worst came to the worst, in a week, Master Quadehar would come looking for them. And each and every one of his friends had a good head on their shoulders.

Comforted by these thoughts, Robin allowed his gaze to roam the sky. He was taken aback, for although he recognized the stars, they were all in the wrong positions. It was very weird. There were the same constellations as on The Lost Isle, but they had slightly different shapes. ... He promised himself he would write down all these observations in his notebook, when he woke up, but for now, exhausted by the day's events, he sank into a deep sleep.

❧

Robin set off the next morning after a restless night filled with frightening dreams in which Amber was calling out to him to help her, and then disappearing before he could do anything. The memory of these nightmares had tormented him since he opened his eyes. He knew that the situation wasn't brilliant, in fact it was a real mess, and his friends might be in serious danger somewhere in the terrible realm of The Uncertain World.

An animal resembling a hare bounded across his path. There was something absurd about its frantic leaps that momentarily brought a smile to Robin's lips. It suddenly dawned on him that he was hungry. And no wonder! The sun was high in the sky and he guessed it was around midday. He reached into his rucksack for a hunk of bread and his fingers closed around the medallion Thomas had given him. He was unable to explain why but, suddenly, he felt as if a great weight had been lifted from his chest. He was able to breathe more easily. Following the lead of the medallion was the obvious thing to do, and the choice of Ferghana as the starting point for his mission seemed to be the only sensible option. He took a bite of the bread and set off again almost joyfully, cheered by the hope that he would soon be reunited with his friends.

Robin had been walking for two days across an extraordinary range of hills. Now he understood why they were described on the map as 'Moving'. The wind that blew his chestnut hair also rippled through the long grass carpeting the hills, and it looked as though the hills were moving, like waves. The sun wasn't as hot as he had feared and the nights were cool rather than cold. But his food supplies had dwindled rapidly, and he knew that he would be in trouble if he didn't come within sight of the city of Ferghana very soon.

However, Robin wasn't really worried. He'd been frequently checking his location on the map, which showed Ferghana's land, air and astronomical coordinates, so he knew that he wasn't far away now. Over and over again, he thanked his master for having forced him to immerse himself in these daunting sciences. Thanks to Quadehar's teaching, thanks to the experience he'd acquired in Penmarch and the knowledge of the various currents of The Uncertain World, he knew his exact whereabouts. The breeze, the energy waves he could feel underfoot, and the sun and the stars guided his steps more reliably than a road map.

And sure enough, a little later, from the summit of a hill that stood higher than the others, he saw the ramparts of Ferghana down below.

23

The Infested Sea

Coral finally opened her eyes – which she'd kept tight shut since they'd stepped through The Door – and allowed them to get used to the dark.

She was lying amid the most unbelievable jumble, with mountains of fabrics, china, chests and carved furniture piled higgledy-piggledy. She gazed about her; the roof and walls were of thick canvas, and slits in the side let in the moonlight. Coral guessed she was in a vast tent. She sat up on the wooden floor. Behind her, a fallen door was jammed between a coffee table and a trunk overflowing with silk scarves.

Coral stood up and anxiously looked for the others. Her eye fell on an oil lamp with a copper lip that stood on the corner of a chest by the entrance and gleamed in the darkness. She lit the wick using an old tinderbox lying next to it – a sign that someone came here from time to time. Then she began to search the tent.

'Hey guys! Stop trying to frighten me, it's not funny!

Come on, show yourselves.... Oooh!'

Lifting a curtain that lay in a heap on the floor, she uncovered a rust-eaten metal chest filled with jewels.

'Whoever left jewels lying around in a place like this must be mad. They're gorgeous!'

Unable to resist, she selected a few and looked around for a mirror, which she found on a dressing table that was warped from the damp. She hung two blue-stone earrings from her ears, and put on a gold necklace and a silver bracelet.

'I look a fright,' she muttered.

From her bag she took out the brush she had insisted on bringing and carefully restyled her hair. Then she continued her search for the others.

She told herself that they'd probably gone outside already. Without waiting for her! She pursed her lips. This wasn't the first time. ... She glanced at her Virdu cloak and shrugged. There was no way she was going to wear something so ugly. In any case, it was dark outside. She opened the canvas flaps.

'Wow! Oh, wow!'

Coral couldn't believe her eyes. She was at sea. Or at least, the sea was sparkling all around her under the crescent moon. She was on a wide platform, like a big raft. And everywhere she looked there were other rafts linked together by wooden gangways. Small waves lapped pleasantly against the planks of wood.

'Amber! Robin! Godfrey! Romaric!'

Without venturing out of the tent, she called her friends in as loud a whisper as she dared muster. There was no answer ... she went back to lie down in the spot where she had opened her eyes, collecting some thick fabrics on the way to make a comfortable mattress and a blanket. She needed to think, but she was tired and cold and needed to rest for a moment.

Why was she alone? Coral was apprehensive. Robin had pointed to an island on the map saying – his confident voice still rang in her ears – '*This is where we'll land in The Uncertain World, just here...*' Huh! A raft might be surrounded by water, but it wasn't an island! She'd been sure it would all go wrong. Hadn't she said so to the others? It was all very well them laughing at her every time she got worried, but, wherever they all were right now, they must be kicking themselves for not listening to her for once. She'd have words with them when she found them. Getting angry now wouldn't solve anything though. ... They'd probably gone to check out the other rafts. The most logical thing she could do was to stay where they must have left her.

Coral rolled herself up in the makeshift blanket and tried to go to sleep. But the gentle rolling motion bothered her, and the sound of the waters lapping against the wooden raft made her jump several times. She could see she was going to have difficulty getting to sleep. She started to think about her mother, in their village of Krakal, about her father, and Amber. Where could she be right now? She would have given anything to hear her sister's nagging at that very moment. Tears ran down her cheeks. What if her friends hadn't arrived at the same point in The Uncertain World?

Eventually, as Coral became accustomed to the splashing of the water, it lulled her and she finally fell asleep. It was already far into the night.

ᴄ

'Look, Daddy, I told you I saw a light and heard a noise coming from the storage tent last night!'

Coral opened her eyes. She was curled up in the same spot, but outside, the sun had replaced the stars. Someone had just spoken. She wasn't dreaming. ...

'What are you doing here?'

Coral sat up in her temporary bed. She saw a little girl and a man standing staring at her.

'I said, what are you doing here? Do you not understand Ska?'

The man's tone was not unkind; he simply looked bewildered. Coral stared back at him for a moment before answering. He wasn't very tall, and he wore only a pair of baggy shorts. His skin was tanned and leathery from the hot and salty sea air. He had an amazing shock of almost white hair, and glassy eyes. The little girl looked remarkably like him.

'Yes, I understand Ska. But I can't explain what I'm doing here. ...'

The little girl, also with long white hair, wore a flimsy tunic over some sort of swimsuit. She was tugging at her father's arm. 'Leave her alone, Daddy. I bet she's a Pachahn. Oh! Please, can I keep her with me?'

The man smiled affectionately at his daughter. 'All right, Matsi. But only until the next coast; you know the rules.'

The man with the weatherbeaten face left the tent. His daughter, who looked about ten years old, came joyfully over to Coral. 'I'm Matsi!'

'And I'm Coral. ... Matsi, your father isn't angry with me, is he?'

'No,' replied the little girl with a big smile. 'Pachahns often climb onto our rafts to hide, when we are close to the shore. But they always get caught!'

'What are the Pachahns?'

'Stowaways, of course! Come on, let's go and play outside. When we reach a coast, you'll be taken ashore and I'll be all on my own again.'

She took Coral's hand and dragged her outside the tent.

'Why are your eyes so light? They look as though they have an extra layer of skin over them.'

Tired of chasing each other and laughing and splashing about in the water, Coral and Matsi were sitting on the edge of the raft, chatting as they dried themselves in the sun. Coral was pleased to have company and playing with the little girl had distracted her from her troubles.

'That's so we can see underwater. Daddy explained to me that all the People of the Sea are born that way.'

'Are there many of you?' asked Coral who'd been fascinated to explore the eighteen rafts of the Sixth Tribe of the People of the Sea, the clan that Matsi and her father belonged to.

'There are thirty tribes altogether,' declared Matsi with pride. Some have forty rafts. In my grandfather's day, ours had twenty-seven! It's better to have a lot of rafts. It's more stable at sea. There are more places to play, too.'

'Don't you ever go ashore?' asked Coral in surprise. 'Do you spend your whole life on your rafts?'

'What would we do on land?' replied Matsi. 'We go close to the shore, that's all. Sometimes, we untie a raft and send it to a beach, to trade our fish for other things. Dry land is dangerous. We're safe here. The only thing is, I've got no one to play with.'

'Haven't you got any friends? Aren't there other children on the rafts?'

'Yes, there are,' replied the little girl with an air of seriousness. 'But my father is the Keeper of the Salvaged Objects and the others don't want to play with me.'

'They don't want to play with you because your father is an important man?' asked Coral, confused.

Matsi burst out laughing and splashed her feet in the water. 'My father, an important man? No, it's the opposite, he's the least important of all! Pachiak, who steers our rafts from coast to coast is an important man. Haliak, who catches the biggest fish of all is an important man. Ousnak, who's a fast swimmer and can swim vast distances, is an important man, but my father, Wal, only guards the things the sea gives us or that Ousnak brings back from the deep. Why would he be important? He guards the stuff that is of no use.'

Coral sat there speechless. Those precious objects, useless? But how could they be ...? She tried to find arguments to convince Matsi of their importance, but, funnily enough, couldn't think of a single one. It was obviously pointless going on about the pleasure of pretty clothes and jewellery in this environment where everyone was half naked! In the end, she asked, 'Why do you keep them then, if they're useless?'

'Because we've always kept them. Just as there's always been a Guide for our rafts, there's always been a Keeper of the Salvaged Objects, it's as simple as that.'

'And does it bother your that your father has that job?'

'What bothers me is that the others don't want to play with me. ... Look, over there! Stingers!'

Matsi pointed towards a huge dark patch floating on the surface, tossed by the waves.

'Are they dangerous?' asked Coral anxiously.

'No, as long as you stay on the raft and keep out of the water.'

The rafts were soon right in the middle of the frightening dark patch. None of the tribe seemed concerned, but everyone was careful not to go too close to the edge.

'They're like ... jellyfish!' exclaimed Coral, who was watching the dense, slimy mass with disgust. 'Uuugh! I hate jellyfish!'

She felt a cold shiver run down her spine. She couldn't help it – she hated anything jelly-like. When she was little, to annoy her, Amber used to chase her with a plate of wobbly redcurrant jelly; Coral would scream until their mother came to the rescue. She had no idea where this disgust had come from. It wasn't her fault, she just couldn't rid herself of it.

'They're Stingers,' Matsi corrected her. 'On their own,

they're not dangerous, but together they can kill a whale! In the old days, they got rid of Pachahns by throwing them to the Stingers,' she added with a laugh. 'Now we show mercy; we just take them ashore when we go to the coast to trade.'

'Urrgh!' shivered Coral. 'It must be horrible if you fall in.'

'You'd die within minutes,' stated Matsi matter-of-factly. 'Your only chance would be to dive down and escape them by swimming under water.'

'Does it work?'

'Yes. I did it once.'

Coral shot her a look of admiration.

'It's easier than getting away from a Gommon, in any case,' added Matsi.

Coral wasn't convinced, and thought she'd rather face one of those monsters than these horrid gooey creatures!

'Do the Gommons come out this far?' she asked.

'No. When they attack us, it's near the coast, or on the beaches.'

'I know that only too well,' muttered Coral, her face clouding over.

The memory of the capture of the Gommon and Agatha's kidnapping – the events that had sparked off this whole adventure – chased the jellyfish from her mind. She thought about her sister and her friends, and was suddenly sad all over again. But what was the point of allowing herself to mope? As she'd told herself over and again, until she was on dry land, there was nothing she could do.

'What's up?' asked Matsi, concerned to see tears glistening in her new friend's eyes.

'Nothing,' replied Coral, fighting back her sadness and shaking her head. 'Let's go and see your father. He's waving to us.'

The smell of barbecued fish that had been wafting in their direction for a while was irresistible, and Matsi's father was calling them to come and eat.

24

The Purple Forest

It must have been early afternoon. For about an hour now, Amber had been continually looking over her shoulder – she had the feeling that someone was following her. She was aware of a presence behind her, and had the nasty feeling someone was watching her. But, whenever she looked round, she saw nothing. She carried on walking under the huge trees, but could not shrug off her anxiety.

The night before, like Robin on his hill and Coral on her raft, Amber had found herself surrounded by darkness. Without panicking, she had waited until her eyes became accustomed to it. A little later, she had been able to make out giant, motionless shapes all around her and, above her head, the moon, masked by heavy, moving clouds.

She walked over to one of the shapes, reached out and gingerly touched it. The familiar feel of rough bark told her it was a tree. 'So, I'm in a forest,' she said to herself with relief, 'that's why it's so dark.'

Looking around her, she fast became aware that her companions weren't with her. She searched and called for them long and hard but there was no denying it, she was completely alone. Amber knew that despite the panic rising up inside her, worrying was pointless. Instead she had to do something about her predicament. But she was unable to suppress a deep sigh. What *had* happened? Nothing good, that was for sure. Perhaps Robin had been wrong and there were several Doors to The Uncertain World? But weren't there magic words to keep them together during the journey?

'I'll have to find that wretched apprentice sorcerer and ask him!' she grumbled.

Then, she pictured her sister, perhaps also alone in front of a door, completely distraught. She clenched her fists determinedly. 'If anyone dares to harm her! Oh! Robin, Robin. ... Why?'

She was furious at herself for having trusted Robin blindly, and she was furious at herself for having urged the others to follow him! But it was no use wallowing in self-pity. She thrust out her chin defiantly and, hands on her hips, she took stock of her surroundings.

❧

Eventually Amber came across the door through which she had arrived, carved into the trunk of a huge oak. As it was too dark now to venture into the forest to explore, she clambered up to the lowest branch that looked strong enough to support her and found a snug place to rest wrapped up in her Virdu cloak.

'At least I'll be safe from wild animals, if there are any!'

Amber wasn't afraid. After one last thought for her sister, she dropped off to sleep, exhausted by the efforts of the day.

At daybreak, she opened her sleepy blue eyes. During the night, she had woken up several times. She'd heard a strange noise at the foot of the tree and, later, she had felt something brush against her. She hadn't been worried, knowing that the forest came to life at night and slept by day. On wakening, she had been greeted by the twittering of the birds, and she stretched lazily as she sat on her branch, swinging her legs.

Then she clambered to the top of the oak and immediately saw that she was in the heart of the forest; there were trees and more trees, as far as the eye could see. She slid down the trunk, landing nimbly on the ground. A glance at the map of The Uncertain World told her that she was most probably in the region of the Purple Forest. Wherever she was, she needed to head due west.

'First of all I've got to get out of here and find a village where I can ask my way and think about how I'm going to find the others,' she concluded.

She noted the position of the sun, and set off westwards. After a while, she once again had the feeling someone was following her.

She walked on for a long time, unable to rid herself of the unpleasant sensation that she was being watched. The old oaks creaked, their branches reaching up above her like the vault of a cathedral. She liked this forest, it reminded her of the Forest of Pamperol, on The Lost Isle, where she often went for walks with her father. Amber was always happy surrounded by nature, especially woodland. On The Lost Isle, there weren't any man-made forests like there were in The Real World. They were all wild, mysterious and full of many strange and wonderful beasts. Any human venturing into them was just another creature among many. There was respect and even a certain harmony between nature and the inhabitants of The Lost Isle. It was like an ancient pact, agreed so long ago that no human memory stretched back that far.

Amber soon reached the edge of a vast open glade. Charred pieces of wood and a ruined hut indicated that charcoal burners had stayed there earlier in the year. Amber ventured into the glade, relieved at discovering signs of a human presence. Then her instincts warned her to be careful. She froze and felt the blood drain from her face. How stupid of her! She must go back into the shelter of the forest, and quickly! If it was an animal that had been following her all this time, then why hadn't it attacked her yet? Had the trees had been protecting her? They could provide her with refuge. She retraced her steps and began to run. But it was too late. ... A huge animal emerged from the fringes of the forest and rushed towards her, growling ferociously. It had the body and trotters of a wild boar, and a dog's head! It was followed by a pack of similarly terrifying creatures. Amber turned and ran screaming towards the abandoned charcoal burner's hut. She stooped to pick up a stick and then scrambled up onto the roof of wobbly beams.

A few seconds later, the hut was surrounded by baying beasts. They drooled, barked and bared their fangs.

'Go away. Lie down! In your basket!' ordered Amber in a terrified voice, threatening them with her stick.

She blinked back her tears. What's the use of crying? The only thing that mattered now was to fight for her life at all costs.

'Come on doggies, come and feel my stick! Go away you horrid pigs, get out!' she cried.

At that moment the leader of the pack launched himself onto the roof and advanced gingerly towards Amber wobbling unsteadily on the narrow beams. She whacked him hard on the nose with her stick, with all the force she could muster, and he fell down through the roof to the rubble below.

'One down! Who's next?'

The animals howled. In a few minutes, they would all attack the hut. Amber knew what was coming, but oddly felt no fear. Only excitement and a fierce determination to fight to the end, until her strength gave out! Suddenly, the sound of a horn rang out and horsemen burst into the glade. Furious at seeing their game was over, the beasts hesitated and then bolted for the forest. The men on horseback rode over to the hut where Amber sat astride a beam, still brandishing her stick.

There were about ten of them, wearing light armour with a purple sheen; the crests of their helmets were made from the skulls of forest animals. They carried hunting spears slung over their shoulders and swords at their sides. Their horses were thickset and sturdy. Some of them had the carcass of an animal similar to a stag slung over their hindquarters. The rider who appeared to be the leader dismounted, and the others immediately followed suit, kneeling down before him.

He walked towards Amber and removed his helmet, which bore a bear skull.

'A woman!' exclaimed Amber, dropping her stick in astonishment.

A mane of long blonde hair tumbled down as the horsewoman took off her helmet to reveal a beautiful face lit up by brilliant green eyes.

'My name is Kushumai. Kushumai the Huntress,' she said, speaking in Ska.

She held her hand out to Amber and helped her down from her unsteady perch.

'And I'm Amber. Amber Krakal. ...'

The Huntress smiled at her and went on, still in Ska, 'Well, Amber, welcome to the fearsome heart of the Purple Forest!'

The young woman, whose companions appeared to be devoted to her, had invited Amber to clamber up behind her on her horse. They had been riding for at least an hour in silence.

Amber decided to break it. There were too many things she was bursting to know. 'Excuse me, my lady, but ... where are we going?'

'Call me Kushumai. I told you my name, earlier. You

are entitled to use it.'

'I'm sorry, er, Kushumai ... but, where are we going?'

'Home to my castle, the Castle of Gor.' Kushumai answered casually.

But Amber wanted to know more, so she continued bombarding the huntress with questions. 'Were you hunting when you heard the monsters barking?'

'Yes. They're called Roukhs, and they're not exactly quiet!'

'And where do these ... Roukhs come from?'

'From the towns, where they're trained to fight. The winners are pampered, and the losers killed, or abandoned in the forests to survive on their own.'

'You mean they're not wild?'

'They're poor creatures, created by unscrupulous magicians. They carry within them the folly of man and that's why they're wicked. The world of nature is hard, sometimes cruel, but it is not wicked. Nature is neither good nor bad. It is beyond the notions of good and evil.'

Amber mulled over Kushumai's words for a moment, then said, 'Lucky you were riding past. You should have seen me running away from the glade in a panic!'

'But we did see you,' replied Kushumai softly.

Amber was bewildered. 'You ... you saw me? So you were there?'

'From the start,' the horsewoman broke in.

'Why? But why?' stammered Amber.

'Because we wanted to see whether you were worth rescuing,' explained the huntress, with a smile. 'If you had given up, if you'd allowed the Roukhs to get the better of you, they'd have enjoyed a good dinner and have deserved it. Only, you didn't give up, you fought back and that's why I wanted to come and help you. Luckily for you!'

'That's outrageous!' protested Amber.

'I told you,' concluded Kushumai in a gentle but firm voice, 'like Mother Nature, my mother, I'm beyond good and evil.'

The Huntress spurred on her steed and they rode on in silence, through the tall trees.

25

The beach

Romaric could feel sand underfoot. He opened his eyes wide and peered into the gloom, just as Robin, Coral and Amber were doing at that same moment.

The first thing he saw was a vast beach enclosed by rocks. The second was the top of a door poking out of the sand, lapped by the waves. And thirdly, he saw that he was alone. He swore under his breath as he paced up and down to try and calm himself. Just wait till he got his hands on that crazy cousin of his, he'd make him sorry he'd ever wanted to be a sorcerer! He'd been wrong earlier, back on The Lost Isle – Robin wasn't just mad, he was also dangerous!

Suddenly, Romaric heard a noise coming from the far end of the beach. What a relief! There he was fretting, and all the while his friends had been just a few metres away, worrying about him and probably looking everywhere for him! He was about to race over to them, but his instinct warned him to be wary. Supposing it wasn't the others? But who else could be wandering along the beach in The Uncertain World in the middle of the night? He held his breath. There was only one answer: Gommons.

Here in The Uncertain World, Gommons would almost certainly be found by the sea at this hour, because ... that was where they lived! Romaric stifled another curse. He hastily covered up his footprints in the sand and walked down by the water's edge, taking care not to splash. He was heading for the rocks at the other end of the beach, but it seemed to be taking forever to get there.

At last Romaric reached the rocks without mishap and then looked about him carefully to make sure there was nothing or nobody lurking behind a boulder. Soon he found a hiding place, a little cave set in a giant rock. He took off his shoes, socks and trousers, which were soaked up to the knees. Then he wrapped himself in his snug Virdu cloak and lay down on the ground.

A little further along the beach, the waves crashed relentlessly against the shore, leaving trails of foam as they retreated. But the sound of the sea did not soothe Romaric. He couldn't sleep, he was too anxious. His mind was buzzing. His thoughts went from his parents to his Uncle Urian, from Urian to Robin, and from Robin to the rest of his friends. He didn't doze off until dawn, and then he slept fitfully, waking up every time a large wave pounded the shore.

‎༺

The sun was already high when Romaric awoke. He dressed, pulling a face at the feel of his damp clothes.

Then he had a bite to eat. His provisions were dwindling and he knew he should just have a snack, but he also knew he couldn't start the day on a half-empty stomach, especially after a night like that. So went ahead and ate all he had, then took a good look outside before leaving his shelter and venturing onto the beach.

He went over to the door, half-buried in the sand. His heart missed a beat. There was a new set of tracks in the spot where he had paced up and down the night before, cursing. And those huge, deep prints were not human.

'So it was Gommons,' murmured Romaric.

He'd had a narrow escape! Romaric had heard terrifying tales of these monsters and their eating habits. They had no qualms about devouring humans, given the chance. He shuddered. Once again, his instincts had saved him.

'Romaric, my friend, you'd better not hang around here,' he said to himself.

Turning his back to the sea, he scrambled up the dunes and, half an hour or so later, he was walking along the edge of a cornfield.

A little further on, he met two elderly farmers sheltering from the sun's first rays under a tree. They were drinking from a gourd. The two men stared at him without looking particularly surprised.

Romaric ran a hand through his hair to tidy it up and started conversing in Ska. He soon learned that he was north of the city of the priests of Yenibohor. A town that was apparently better to avoid when you were young and healthy, because, as legend had it, the priests were famed for rapid conversions and frequent sacrifices.

'But you probably know that only too well, my boy?' The man winked at his companion.

'Why would I know that?' asked Romaric carefully.

'Oh!' replied the second farmer smiling. 'It's not the first time a novice has run away from that dreadful place to seek refuge on the coast.'

'There is much that we see, but our lips are sealed. Why should we help those wicked priests? It's bad enough having to pay them tithes,' he said, for the benefit of his comrade.

'No reason to tell them anything,' agreed the other, nodding. 'On the other hand, there's no reason why we shouldn't give you a word of advice, my boy. Go back to the sea shore and wait for a boat to come, then wave.'

'But what about the Gommons?' objected Romaric.

'The Gommons are preferable to the men of Yenibohor,' explained the first farmer. 'And you'll always stand a better chance of escaping by sea than over land – the white-robed priests control the entire peninsula.'

The two men offered him some wine diluted with water from their gourd and a hunk of bread to eat. Romaric took it gladly. Still chewing the huge doorstep they'd cut him, he decided to follow the farmers' advice.

He was about to thank them warmly and bid them goodbye before retracing his steps, when he remembered the medallion Thomas had shown them all just before they went through The Door. He drew the symbol pictured on it in the dirt. The two men exchanged glances.

'It's the coat of arms of the city of Yadigar, which is

south of the Ravenous Desert. It is said to be a bad place. Is that where you come from?'

'No, that's where I think I must be meant to go. ... You seem to be very knowledgeable for simple farmers!' said Romaric in surprise.

'Is that an insult or a compliment?' laughed the two men. 'Do you imagine that people who till the soil and look after animals are all stupid?'

'No,' stammered Romaric, 'No ... I meant you seem to have travelled a lot, that's all!'

'You don't necessarily need to travel to be educated,' stated the first farmer. 'You learn a bit in school, a lot from books, and even more from life!'

'And from the stories of those who have travelled!' guffawed the other.

Romaric said a heartfelt goodbye and then set off back along the path to the beach.

Romaric wasn't happy to see the beach again, but at least it was still deserted. He knew that he should be cautious and hide among the rocks, but he hated waiting and patience wasn't one of his virtues. So he passed the time by doing exercises to loosen up, and by practising his Quwatin – the martial art used on The Lost Isle. Then he walked along the shore for a while. In the distance, he could see a stretch of land that could have been an island and, above it, a fiery mountain that must be a volcano. He was desperate to explore. He'd never be able to stay on this beach. Besides, how long could he hold out? Even with what the farmers had given him, he only had two days' worth of provisions left. He made up his mind there and then. He'd wait two days for a ship to appear. After that, he'd try his luck over land, and blast the priests of Yenibohor! He preferred to risk his life by trying to do something, rather than to lose it stupidly by doing nothing.

Romaric went back to the cave where he had spent the night and pored over the map of The Uncertain World, copied in better times on the beloved Lost Isle, surrounded by his friends.

26

A feat of strength

Godfrey took a few steps forward. Torches were burning, held in iron brackets protruding from the walls, their flickering light illuminating the blood-red wall hangings of a vast round room. The place was crammed with shelves bowed under the weight of books and maps, and there were tables covered with test tubes, some of which were being heated by gas lamps, the liquid inside them boiling and bubbling.

'Welcome to the Evil Sorcerer's den!' thought Godfrey gazing about him. In the centre of the room was a door just like the one they had gone through on The Lost Isle.

'Five of us went through The Door, and now I'm all alone on the other side', Godfrey said to himself.

He folded his arms, then scratched his chin with his right hand, looking puzzled, as he always did when he was lost in thought.

One thing was certain – Robin's spell had worked. There was no doubt that he was now on the other side of The Door in a strange room. But something had obviously gone wrong, since he was apparently all alone in this frightening place.

Magic was probably very much like music – if you were just one semitone out, you ended up playing a different tune from the one you meant to play! Or, if you played a piece in the wrong key ...

Yes, that was probably what had happened: they had all approached the same piece in a different key! Why? He was no sorcerer, but he knew the mistake would have to be remedied and the instruments tuned so they could all play in harmony. In a nutshell, they had to find each other.

He went over to a metal door, which led to a spiral staircase. Suddenly, he stopped dead. He could hear sounds coming from the staircase, noises that were getting louder. There was no doubt about it, someone was climbing the steps.

Without panicking, Godfrey cast about for another exit. Peering through the dark, he eventually made out a window on the opposite side of the room. The flame of the torch on the wall to the right of it flickered in the slight draught, indicating that it was a window to the outside. Without wasting another moment, Godfey raced over to it. The window was barely big enough for him to slip through. He didn't have a second to worry about how far up he would find himself. He had to hurry as the sound of footsteps on the stairs was getting closer. Luckily, he found himself in a narrow casement rather than on a ledge, but it was so cramped that he was forced to go down on all fours and crawl. He inched forward, using the rough stones to help him, until finally he reached the open air.

It was night. The stars twinkled in the sky, and a pale moon lit up a rocky mass ... about twenty metres below! Further down still was the sea shore, and he could hear the waves crashing against the foot of a cliff. Feeling giddy, with his heart pounding against his ribcage, Godfrey closed his eyes. Amber and Romaric were the brave ones who should have been here, not him. They were both adventurous climbers and didn't know the meaning of fear!

He took several deep breaths to calm himself down before opening his eyes again. Then he saw that he was just below the top of a tower. He couldn't go back into the room, so he had two options: either stay put and hide until the owners of the footsteps left the room – which could be a while – or climb to the top of the tower. The horror of having to overcome his fear of heights made him turn back. He crawled back the way he had come and, hidden by the surrounding darkness, peered into the room. He could see someone clearly. A man was very busy at one of the tables covered in various magical-looking instruments. He had his back turned, but Godfrey could make out that he was tall and thin. At one point, he held a test tube up to the light of a torch to examine the contents and Godfrey saw with a shock that the man was missing a finger on his right hand.

Then Godfrey heard another set of footsteps on the staircase. A heavy tread, so obviously terrifying that

Godfrey decided to try his luck outside after all, without waiting to find out more. He groped his way back to the end of the casement as fast as he could.

With his face against the wall, he began to extricate himself, his arms stretched out above him, desperately seeking something to grab on to. He felt the outline of a metal ring. Suddenly, he found himself dangling in mid-air, his whole body flattened against the outside wall.

'I must be totally mad!' he groaned. He had never been so frightened in his life.

Slowly and painfully, taking great care not to look down, he managed to heave himself slowly up by holding onto the ring, and finally reached the top of the tower. He climbed over the parapet, then, exhausted, he dropped down onto the paved floor. 'I can't imagine why Amber thinks climbing's fun. ...' he thought, shaking his head.

Now, he was faced with the challenge of finding some other way of leaving this wretched tower!

It didn't take him long to get his breath back and within a few moments he was able to muster his strength. He swiftly inspected the platform he'd reached. The only visible way down was a spiral staircase that led into the building. But that was out of the question, for he was sure that was where the menacing sound of footsteps had come from. He grimaced and leaned over the parapet, and was relieved to discover another solution – a series of beams protruding from the wall, spiralling down to the base of the tower. He imagined that they had probably been used when the tower was being built.

Taking his courage in both hands, Godfrey stepped onto the first beam, keeping as close to the wall as he could.

The descent felt as if it would never end. He kept having to stop to use his sleeve to wipe the perspiration that was dripping down his forehead and stinging his eyes. By the time he finally reached the ground, he was trembling from head to foot.

When he had recovered, he saw that in front of him a little path ran down between two giant rock formations. Godfrey rushed headlong down it, passing the ruins of what must once have been a fortified village – gaping houses, crumbling walls. He ran until he was breathless. At last, when he was sure he was safe, he stopped. Adjusting his Virdu cloak, he turned around and gazed at the dark, menacing tower rising up into the sky. He shuddered, and continued on his way.

27

Magic Tricks

Robin arrived at the foot of the walls of Ferghana as the setting sun bathed the city in an intense ochre glow. Being close to the Sea of Great Winds and the Ravenous Desert, Ferghana was an important trade centre. It had once been a staging post on the Forest Road, which, in more affluent times, had channelled the natural wealth of the Purple Forest towards the affluent cities of the south. But today, the city owed its opulence to its markets, which attracted people from all over The Uncertain World, and to the taxes the city authorities imposed on those who went there to do business.

Disguised in his Virdu cloak, Robin presented himself at one of the monumental gates of the fortified city. To gain admittance, he had to pay a toll of one emerald and two sapphires to a hideous-looking guard, clearly a cross between an Ork and a human.

Robin wandered aimlessly through the winding streets. The air was filled with a strong aroma – a combination of stew, washing and urine. He was fascinated by the array of glittering merchandise displayed on the stalls and by the side-shows of jugglers and fire-eaters that entertained the crowds thronging the narrow streets. Making his way to the centre of the city, concealed under his grey cloak, he passed a few Orks and other strange creatures; however, the population was mostly made up of human beings.

His footsteps led him to a huge square. It was crowded and noisy. He spent a small gemstone on some food which he bought from a makeshift stall made up of grimy tables under a shabby awning, sandwiched between a bear-tamer and a salesman extolling the virtues of a miracle ointment. He bit into a huge leg of batachul – a sort of big pheasant from the Moving Hills – stuffed with kutsis – peppery mushrooms from the mountains of Virdu. He found the stuffing horribly hot, so, to take the edge off the fieriness, gulped down some sharap, a sweet wine from the Middle Islands. But the wine quickly went to his head and made him feel tipsy. He wisely decided to round off his meal with a palaur, a red apple from the eastern regions of The Uncertain World. Finally satisfied, he stood up and set off to explore once again.

A little further along, a group of children was crowding around the wagon of a man in a colourful costume. He wore a long blue robe covered in stars and on his head, a tall, pointed hat.

'... and now, I, Gordogh, the greatest magician in the world, am going to make this ball vanish!'

The man shook his hand with the most astonishing speed and the ball he was holding vanished. The children let out an 'Ooohh!' of delight.

'A conjuror!' said Robin to himself with a smile. The man was skilful. He made several objects disappear and then reappear behind the ear of an incredulous spectator.

Then he raised his arms to request silence and announced, 'And now, the great Gordogh will make one of you disappear. ...'

He scanned the crowd for a volunteer. The children all looked away and tried to make themselves as inconspicuous as possible. His gaze fell on Robin. 'You, Little Man of Virdu! Come up here and join me!'

Propelled forward by eager hands, Robin found himself standing before Gordogh. The conjuror made him take a step back to the left. Then, with a look of satisfaction, he addressed the audience, 'By the power of the ancestral skull, I possess the all-powerful Force! I have the power to make you vanish. Go!'

Swirling his cloak to conceal Robin from the audience, the magician walked in front of him and pressed a button with his foot. Robin heard a click, a trap door beneath him opened and he tumbled down underneath the covered wagon. Immediately, he felt himself being grabbed by two men.

'Come on, Little Man, give us your precious stones and your cloak, or kiss the world goodbye!'

Robin struggled in vain. He called the Graphems to his aid. They took a while to appear, but when he invoked Thursaz, the Mountain, it was Isaz, the Brilliant, that came instead. All the signs were quivering, and Robin found it difficult to recognize them. It was very puzzling! He tried desperately to invoke the help of the Graphem of Defence, but failing miserably and just before being hit over the head by his attackers, he murmured the name of the Graphem of Immobility and Self-Control, 'Isaaaaz. ...'

Suddenly the grip on his body seemed to relax. He was astounded to find the sham magician's two accomplices lying on the ground, completely frozen! He shivered. Above him, he could still hear Gordogh entertaining the audience with his conjuring tricks, probably to give his accomplices the time to finish their job. Robin crawled to the back of the wagon and ran into the narrow streets of Ferghana.

Something bizarre had happened to his magic! OK, he knew what had gone wrong on the journey from The Lost Isle – he'd forgotten one of the Graphems in his Galdr. It was stupid, it shouldn't have happened and, because of his mistake, he and his friends were separated. But it made sense. There was a logical explanation. But why hadn't the Graphems behaved properly when he'd called them? That did sometimes occur, as a result of tiredness or lack of concentration. But he hadn't been able to stop them quivering, which he'd always been able to do until now! And why had he had such trouble recognizing them? They had been all distorted! He'd called Thursaz, which had refused to appear, and Isaz had turned up instead. Why? OK, it wasn't the first time that the Graphems had acted on their own initiative, beyond his control. But then how come those guys had ended up frozen? Isaz was supposed to affect him, not them! Of course he remembered that Master Quadehar had warned him that the Graphems behaved differently in The Uncertain World. But he wasn't prepared for this! How was he going to learn to control them here?

Robin promised himself that he wouldn't use any more magic in The Uncertain World until he understood what was going on.

Then he turned his attention to the signs on the shop fronts.

He soon found what he was looking for. In a little lane, standing on its own, was a jeweller's shop that was still open. The dim light from an oil lamp fell onto the cobbles. He pushed open the door.

At the back of the shop there was an old man sitting at a workbench, his glasses on the end of his nose and several watches in pieces before him. Sitting at his feet on the ground, a young boy handed him the instruments that he needed.

'What do you want?' he asked gruffly in Ska.

'I want to know where this medallion comes from,' replied Robin, also in Ska, holding out the silver object Thomas had given him just before he went through The Door.

The jeweller snatched the medallion and turned it over and over between his fingers. 'No idea. Now be off with you. I'm closing.' Then he turned to the young boy. 'Kyle, see the Little Man to the door and double-bolt it.'

The boy got up. He looked about the same age as

Robin. He was thin and wiry, and his blue eyes contrasted with his dark hair and tanned skin. His bare feet were shackled by a heavy chain which made him hobble awkwardly. He showed Robin out, as the jeweller had asked him to do, but before he left, the boy whispered, ' Meet me in one hour. At the basement window over the street. ... I can help you.'

The door shut and Robin heard the sound of the bolt being drawn. The light went out almost at once, and Robin found himself in the dark.

28

Romaric takes the plunge

'Wal. ... Can I tell you something?'

Coral had gone over to Matsi's father, who turned to her with a kindly look.

'It's about the jewels I'm wearing. Actually, they're not mine, they're yours ... I found them in the tent. I'm going to give them back to you.'

She removed the blue-stone earrings, the gold necklace and the silver bracelet, and held them, but the man made no move to take them.

'Take them back, Wal. Please! You've been so kind to me from the start. I feel guilty at having ... well, stolen from you.'

She blushed as she said the word 'stolen'. The Keeper of the Salvaged Objects burst out laughing.

'Keep your jewels, my dear. They're much better on you than in our tent! Besides, only you and I know they exist. And even if that weren't the case, who would begrudge you? I wouldn't stop anyone coming and helping themselves from the chests, but nobody ever does.'

Coral gazed directly into Wal's translucent eyes and saw that he was serious. She smiled at him and put the jewellery back on. Wal patted her arm as if to say that was the end of the matter.

Matsi suddenly appeared and rushed over to her father. 'The coast! The coast! Coral's going to be sent ashore now, isn't she?'

To her surprise, Coral saw that the flotilla of rafts was indeed close to the coast. A long beach stretched out before her, broken up by occasional rocks. The little girl began to sob her heart out. 'For the first time I've found a friend, a friend all to myself!'

Wal comforted his daughter. 'No, Matsi, not here. We'll land further south. This coast is infested with Gommons, and the land you see in the distance is that of the priests of Yenibohor. The People of the Sea are not on very good terms with them.'

'Why?' asked Coral.

'Not so long ago, in the days when we still used to barter our fish for their wheat, children used to mysteriously vanish while we were ashore. It's in the past now, but we have long memories. And we're as dogged in our feuds as we are loyal in our friendships.'

Wal seemed to be in a particularly talkative mood.

'You've never told me about your people, Wal,' said Coral, taking advantage of the moment.

'Because there's nothing to say about them, my dear. Well, nothing that makes us any different from any other people or any other creatures. We're born, we live, we die.'

'But why these rafts, why do you live only on water?'

'A long time ago,' Wal, went on, 'the People of the Sea used to live on land, scattered along the coasts of the Infested Sea. There were many of us and we made a living from fishing and selling woven seaweed mats. You could say we were happy. Then one day, the Gommons appeared out of the blue. Perhaps sent by an evil god who didn't like our people. These monsters fought us for the control of the coast. Gommons are fierce, powerful and cruel. We had little chance of defeating them. They killed many of my people.'

Coral turned pale and bit her lip. She knew enough of her own people's history to know that it was the Brotherhood and the Guild that, in the late Middle Ages, had driven out the Gommons from The Lost Isle and sent them into The Uncertain World to get rid of them! Wal misunderstood Coral's distress.

'Yes, it was terrible. ... The village chiefs eventually assembled to discuss the future of our people. We couldn't seek refuge inland, because of the fierce tribes in the interior. But we noticed that although the Gommons are excellent swimmers, they won't stray far from the shore because our sea is swarming with Stingers. Our destiny was obvious – we would find sanctuary on the Infested Sea! So each village built and fitted out huge rafts. When they all put to sea together, there was hardly any clear water in sight. They weren't called tribes then, but villages. Well, there were no less than three hundred villages floating on the sea and being buffeted by the tides. On the rafts were thousands of villagers who knew nothing about navigation! Nowadays, there are only a few hundred of us altogether, divided into thirty tribes. The others perished in the storms, were attacked by sea monsters or were unable to resist the lure of the land where only disaster awaited them.

Coral said nothing. She felt horribly awkward, but couldn't possibly tell Wal that her own ancestors were the unwitting cause of his people's suffering.

'Don't say anything, my dear. I told you earlier – a tribe can perish just like a man! The important thing is to live a good life. Look at us – are we to be pitied? No! We never go hungry, we're never cold and above all, we are as free as Bohik, the sea breeze that blows over the ocean!'

Coral was moved. She smiled gratefully at Wal, who patted her cheek affectionately.

The conversation ended as Matsi, tired of waiting, grabbed Coral's hand and dragged her off to play.

Romaric emerged from the cave where he had been hiding for the last two days. It was the middle of the afternoon and the sun was beating down. He had eaten all his food supplies and had no water left. And still no boat had appeared off the coast. He would have to stick to his plan and leave this beach to try his luck inland.

He surveyed the ocean. To his left, in the distance, he thought he could make out a huge moving mass being tossed around on the waves. Was it an optical illusion?

He couldn't see clearly, and creased his eyes against the glare of the sun and its reflection on the water.

Then his attention was drawn to something bigger, to his right. Perhaps drifting tree trunks or an old wreck. No, they were rafts, he was certain! Romaric scrambled down from the rocks and ran across the sand, shouting and waving. He soon stopped, realizing that nobody could hear him. The rafts were too far away.

But three Gommons had heard him, and were advancing menacingly down the beach towards him.

Romaric hesitated. There was no point going back into the rocks, and he couldn't run across the fields, because the Gommons blocked the way. There was only one solution and not a very good one. He would have to try to reach the rafts out at sea! Without wasting any more time, he ran to the water's edge and dived into a wave.

As soon as he was out of the surf, he launched into a powerful crawl and swam for his life. He kicked hard, convinced that a huge Gommon hand would grab one of his ankles and drag him under at any moment. But when he turned around, he saw that the three monsters were still on the beach, watching him without making a move. Romaric felt a huge surge of relief and took a breath. He headed to his right, towards the rafts, without noticing that the big dark patch he had seen earlier was moving dangerously close to him.

*

'Look over there!' cried Matsi grasping Coral's hand.

'Why, what is it?' replied Coral blinded by the sun.

'There are Gommons on the beach. Can you see them?'

'Yes, there they are, I can see them. They're so ugly! Is it us they're after?'

'I think they're looking at that boy who's swimming towards us. Or at the Stingers that will soon be on top of him.'

'A boy? What boy ! Where? Where Matsi?'

'There,' said the little girl pointing.

At last Coral could make out the figure in the sea. She froze. It couldn't be! But it was!

'Oh no!' she groaned, biting her fingers. 'I can't bear it! Romaric ...'

'Do you know him?' asked Matsi in surprise.

'Yes, of course, it's my friend Romaric!'

'Well your friend's about to die, I think,' the little girl announced matter-of-factly.

The dark shadow was almost on top of Romaric by the time he became aware of the jellyfish shoal. He was tiring, even though the rafts were no more than a few metres away now. And he couldn't help darting terrified looks over his shoulder at the Stingers; their bodies puffing up and deflating, and their tentacles quivering in anticipation.

'They're going to catch him before he reaches the rafts. I must ... no, I can't ... I daren't!' shouted Coral.

She closed her eyes and pictured herself choking in a giant bowl of redcurrant jelly. She shuddered. No way, she just couldn't.

Romaric let out a strangled cry, which hit Coral like an

electric shock and jolted her into action.

As if driven by sudden force, she marched to the edge of the raft.

'What are you doing?' asked Matsi anxiously.

'I'm going to prove, once and for all,' replied Coral in a strained voice and with a forced smile, 'that boys really can't manage without girls.'

Then as the little girl looked on in amazement, Coral dived into the dark waters.

The shock of entering the water made her feel strong again. In a few strokes she had joined Romaric who was now showing signs of exhaustion. When he saw her coming, he swallowed a mouthful of water in surprise and nearly choked. Coral slipped a hand under his chin and supported him while he got his breath back. Behind them, the Stingers were less than a metre away, moving in a dense mass.

'Don't look, don't look', muttered Coral to herself, shuddering. Then she said to the exhausted Romaric, 'Follow me and do exactly as I do!'

'But how? What ...? Why ...?'

'Later. We don't have much time. Are you ready?'

Romaric nodded. Coral took a big gulp of air and dived. He quickly did the same. They swam deep under water towards the rafts for as long as they could. When they came back up for air, they saw that the Stingers had stayed put, clearly confused by their sudden disappearance.

'Come on, Romaric,' cried Coral. 'We're nearly there!'

She dived down again, mentally thanking Matsi for

her valuable advice.

A few minutes later, the strong arms of the men of the Sixth Tribe were pulling the two of them out of the dangerous waters.

29

A music-loving giant

Godfrey walked southwards. Taking the first opportunity to study his copy of the map of The Uncertain World, he decided that the tower he had risked his life escaping from was most probably the Tower of Jaghatel. A childlike drawing of it seemed to be mocking the sea serpent shown in the middle of the Vast Ocean. It made sense to Godfrey to try and follow the trail of Thomas's medallion – the only clue the friends all shared – and he reckoned that it was best to head for Virdu, as all five of them would be wearing Virdu cloaks, in the hope of meeting someone who knew the way.

The road passed through a small village. Godfrey tried to ask the few inhabitants he met about the medallion, marking out a picture of it in the dirt. They all shook their heads as if they had never seen anything like it.

He also drew a blank in the second village he reached that evening. The people, who were short with red hair and milky skin, weren't very talkative, which didn't help.

After polishing off the remains of his provisions, he spent the night curled up in a field, at the foot of a haystack.

The next day, Godfrey had more luck in a third village, which was bigger than the other two, where he stopped mid-morning. He was just bargaining in Ska for a few apples to keep a fat sausage and a round loaf of bread company in his lunch bag, when his gaze fell on the open door of a violin-maker's workshop. Without further ado, he parted with the gemstone the apple grower demanded and rushed over to investigate. It was a real Aladdin's cave! On the walls hung violas, harps and mandolins of every kind, shape and colour imaginable.

The craftsman looked up, stared at the visitor for a moment and then went back to his work. Eventually, he spoke, 'Do you want to buy something?'

Godfrey was startled by his appearance. The man, who was tall and fair-haired, did not look like the other people from the region, who, on the whole, were short with auburn hair. He was probably a traveller, who, for some unfathomable reason, had opened his shop in this remote village.

'Er ... I ...,' replied Godfrey, pulling his Virdu cloak around him, 'I'm just looking. ...'

The violin-maker smiled in amusement. 'Since when were the Little Men of Virdu interested in music?'

'And since when did the local peasants make this kind of instrument?' retorted Godfrey, quick as a flash, before biting his tongue in embarrassment.

The man burst out laughing. Godfrey hesitated, then he too began to laugh. He pushed down his hood and went over to the man.

'You're right, I'm not from Virdu. But you're not from around here, are you?'

The man silenced him with a gesture. 'Everyone has their secrets, my boy. Suppose you tell me what I can do for you?'

Godfrey picked up a gouge and chiselled out the image from Thomas's medallion on a piece of wood – a sort of lion surrounded by flames.

'I'm looking for the place where this symbol can be found.'

The violin-maker looked wary. 'I think it is the coat of arms of Yadigar, a city in the south-east, on the other side of the Ravenous Desert. I travelled far and wide before settling here, but I've never been there. I do know, from hearsay, that it is the haunt of bandits and thieves. Are you really planning to go there, son?'

'Yes,' sighed Godfrey. 'I have friends who I hope are probably waiting for me there.'

'Well, good luck. Only, before you leave, I advise you to pray to your gods; you're likely to need their help.'

The man bade him farewell and returned to his work.

'Wait,' replied Godfrey. Just as he was about to leave, a magnificent zither had caught his eye. 'How much is this beautiful instrument?'

&

Godfrey was soon back on the road, his bag full of food, his new zither slung over his shoulder. From time to time, he stopped, caressed the instrument's smooth edges and plucked a few strings. It had cost him all the remaining precious stones that Robin had given him, but he didn't care. He could always survive by busking! As long as he could find a more receptive audience than grumpy villagers.

His wish was granted that evening. He had turned off towards the south-east, and there seemed to more people on this new road. At nightfall, he came across a merchant's camp with around thirty empty wagons, arranged in a circle to provide protection against attacks by bandits.

The merchants were from Ferghana, a trading centre in the east; they had sold their goods in Virdu and were on their way home, their pockets filled with precious stones. As was customary in The Uncertain World they had called on the services of mercenaries to protect them. In this case, they were mostly Hybrids, a cross between humans and Orks, who bore the hideous signs of their parentage on their bodies and faces.

The merchants did their best to ignore Godfrey until he introduced himself as a strolling zither-player trying to make a living. Even then, the merchants insisted he was searched before he could join them by the big camp fire. Afterwards the Hybrids continued to watch him carefully, marking every move he made.

Godfrey tried to remain calm, but he shuddered at the memory of their huge claws searching him up and down. But he soon cheered himself up by sitting close to the fire among the opulently dressed merchants who were thrilled at the prospect of an evening that promised to be less dull than usual. He sang funny Ska songs of his own composition and made the Ferghana merchants laugh until tears rolled down their cheeks. Then he played a few mournful laments from The Lost Isle which plunged them into a melancholy silence.

It was getting late. The men from Ferghana slipped away, one by one, to go and sleep in their wagons. Godfrey was soon left alone by the fire.

'I've never heard those tunes before. Where do you come from, young minstrel?' One of the mercenaries asked, sitting apart from the others.

He was huge, at least a head taller than his companions when he was standing. His shoulders almost concealed the wheel of the wagon he was leaning against. He wasn't a Hybrid, but a giant of a man, like Urian Penmarch.

'I ... I ... I make them up,' stammered Godfrey.

'You're gifted. Why do you waste your talents on the road, putting your life at risk?'

The giant stood up and walked over to him. He moved with an agility and speed that was astonishing in one so bulky. 'Well? Won't you tell me?'

His voice was measured and resonant and there was no hint of cruelty in his grey eyes, despite his terrifying appearance. His head was bald, with dragons tattooed across the smooth skull, while his torso and arms were covered in the angry scars of his profession.

'The road is the best school for a strolling player, and there's nothing better than being one's own master and sleeping under the stars,' replied Godfrey dreamily, lost in contemplation of the flames.

'A poet's reply,' murmured the giant. 'I like you, kid! In the steppes of the north, where I come from, people love music. The music of the wind in the birches, the whinnying of horses galloping, the patter of the rain on our felt tents. ... We also love the music of words, the tales of our wise elders, the stories our children make up, the women's love poems. ...'

They sat in silence for a moment. Godfrey felt good. Instinctively, he trusted this giant whose soul seemed so enlightened. 'My name's Godfrey. Godfrey Grum.'

'And I'm Tofann.' The giant smiled, revealing his great fangs.

'Where are you heading, Godfrey?'

'I'm going to Yadigar to meet some friends.'

'That's a coincidence, so am I. As soon as we get to Ferghana, I'm taking leave of my employers and making for the City of Fire. They say that Lord Thunku pays the men who serve him handsomely, and that there are opportunities to take part in some fine battles! Let's travel together, young minstrel. You play for me and I'll protect you from harm.'

They shook hands to seal their pact, his fingers, crushed by the giant's. Godfrey mused that Uncle Urian's grip was gentle in comparison.

30

The Huntress

After a long ride, Kushumai and Amber arrived at Gor Castle – which was actually more of an ancient hill fort. Surrounded by massive, sharp wooden stakes, it stood on a man-made mound in the centre of a vast clearing. A stream had been diverted to form a deep moat before continuing its natural course. A drawbridge led to the main door, which opened onto a spacious courtyard surrounded by three long buildings. One was the stables, and the two others housed the dormitory, the kitchen and a great hall – the main living area of the twenty or so men who made up the castle garrison. The battlements formed part of the roof. In the centre of the courtyard stood a square tower, three storeys high. Everything was made of wood.

'I didn't build Gor to protect me from men,' Kushumai explained to Amber on their arrival. 'The forest does that for me! My castle simply discourages hungry or curious animals.'

Kushumai's men greeted their leader joyfully, then led the horses off to feed and water them. Kushumai and Amber went straight to the tower, which the Huntress occupied alone. The ground floor was a store room; in the centre, a deep well provided a permanent supply of cool water. On the first floor was a large room with a corner fireplace made of heavy black metal and supported by stones. This room contained linen chests, a double bed, two large armchairs and a cupboard full of weapons. There were furs spread everywhere.

'The top floor is my place of privacy,' Kushumai warned. 'Nobody apart from me has ever set foot up there, and nobody ever will.'

One of the hunters came and lit the candles of a big candelabra, in the centre of the room. He had changed out of his armour into more comfortable clothes of leather and had exchanged his sword for a dagger.

Kushumai asked for dinner to be brought to them in the tower, and the man nodded and disappeared.

'Sometimes I eat alone here,' the Huntress told Amber who, amazed at everything around her, was lost for words. 'But usually I join my men in the great hall. They like to have me with them.'

Kushumai told her guest how she had arrived in the Purple Forest, desperate, seeking refuge from the pursuit of the fierce monks of Yenibohor. She had angered them by practising rites that were banned on their territory and dancing on the roof of one of their temples under the light of the full moon.

'It's strange,' said the hostess, 'how men are sometimes

afraid of women.'

The forest had hidden the sorceress and given her a home and food. She had then discovered that other people lived in the shelter of the Purple Forest – hermits, fugitive bandits, fake magicians pursued by real sorcerers. ... She had succeeded in conquering them and convincing them that together they would be able to bear the burden of their exile. These were the men Amber had seen around the castle and met in the forest when she had been attacked by the Roukhs. Kushumai told her that they traded furs for weapons and metal. For everything else, they lived off the bounty of the forest. In turn these men had elected Kushumai as the Huntress and their queen! Queen of the Purple Forest.

Amber lay on her stomach daydreaming, her chin resting on the palm of her hand and her eyes wistful. She luxuriated in the warmth of an Ohts fur which was the size of giant bearskin. It was a wonderful story, a true story. She felt a mixture of admiration and envy for her hostess, who was carving slices of grilled meat on the steaming platter they had been brought.

'Come on, don't let yourself starve to death,' said Kushumai holding out a piece of meat on the end of her knife.

Amber took it, burning her fingers, but nevertheless ate ravenously. When she had finished her meal, the Huntress brought a thick blanket.

'Enough excitement for today,' declared her hostess snuffing out the candles. 'It's time to rest. Good night.'

As Kushumai left the room, Amber wanted to protest

– there was so much to talk about, she didn't want to sleep. But she was so tired that, a few minutes later, she was in deep slumber.

*

'Tell me more about your friends,' asked Kushumai, the next morning, as she and Amber were walking in the grove around the castle, looking for mushrooms to have cooked for breakfast.

The previous day, during their ride, Amber had started to tell the Huntress her life story, omitting any mention of The Lost Isle. She had talked at length about the members of her gang, and told Kushumai of their adventures. Afterwards, she wondered, although it was a bit late, whether she had done the right thing, and whether it might have been wise to be more cautious. But Kushumai had listened to her, if not with interest, at least without interrupting her, and she felt that in exchange for her hospitality, it was the least she could do. Besides, what could it possibly matter? Kushumai lived an isolated existence in the Purple Forest, far removed from the affairs of the world.

'First of all there's Coral. She's my sister. She's a bit silly and a scaredy-cat; all she thinks about is clothes and partying. But she's very sweet, very loving and all the boys are crazy about her!'

'Aren't they crazy about you too?' asked Kushumai, amused.

'I don't care about being pretty or about boyfriends. It's more fun winding them up! And showing them I can do anything they can do. Too bad if they're scared of me.

What I want is respect!'

'Is that all you really want? Just to show them that you can do anything they can do? Well, of course, you can! But there is more to life than that. You see, Amber, I can wield a sword as well as the best of my men. I had to, to win their respect. But I also rule them with kindness and love. There is room in this world for both – you'll discover that for yourself one day. Now tell me, are you closer to any one of your friends. What about this Robin you spoke of yesterday?'

Kushumai's words unsettled Amber. She felt vaguely that there might be some truth in them.

'Uh? Oh! Robin. ... At first he used to get on my nerves, he'd go red and start stammering at the slightest thing. Always sighing and daydreaming. But now ... he's different, it's true. He's grown stronger, more sure of himself. He always blushes when we tease him, but not in the same way. There's a new confidence, a mystery about him. I definitely like him even more now.'

'You've got plenty of time to think about that,' said Kushumai with a strange smile. 'You're at the age when you're just beginning to explore your emotions! Let's go back, we've got enough mushrooms to feed an army.'

They reached the castle and broke off the conversation about Amber's friends. Kushumai showed her around the stables. The horses were magnificent. Then she placed a light sword in Amber's hands and taught her a few strokes, much to the amusement of the men pacing the battlements.

It was soon time to light the fires and wait for dinner.

Chatting pleasantly, it occurred to Amber to slip into the conversation the description of the medallion that Thomas had shown them. 'Yadigar,' Kushumai had merely muttered, almost to herself. Amber tried to press her to say more, but her hostess laughed, saying, in a mysterious voice, that she would have an answer to her questions in the morning. Then a hunter arrived with drinks.

'Amber,' announced Kushumai, raising her goblet filled with wine, 'I drink to the future.'

'And I,' echoed Amber, intoxicated with the excitement of this extraordinary day, 'I also drink to fate, for leading you to the grove where I was fighting the Roukhs!'

They clinked goblets.

As soon as she had drunk the wine, Amber's head started swimming. 'But wh ... Kushumai! What is it ...?'

Her head spinning, she crumpled to the floor.

Kushumai hadn't moved a muscle. She raised her glass again and drained it to the last drop. 'To the future, Amber, and to fate!'

Amber briefly came to as Kushumai carried her up to the top floor of the tower. It was crammed with books, herbs in pots and flasks containing indescribable potions.

She awoke a second time when Kushumai laid her on a crude wooden table. She saw, through a haze, the Huntress draw strange signs in the air above her body, and heard her murmur a haunting incantation. Then Amber slipped into unconsciousness once more.

Kushumai applied tremendous concentration. The spell she was imprinting deep inside Amber was complicated. It took her until late into the night. When she had finished, she gazed at the young girl and felt a pang of conscience.

'Forgive me, little Amber,' she whispered. 'I had to do it to protect you. ... Tomorrow, you won't remember a thing.'

She carried Amber down from the tower and into the stables. Her horse was already saddled. She mounted, rode out of the castle gate and galloped towards the forest, with Amber slung in front of her.

Just as dawn was breaking, they reached the door carved into the great oak through which Amber had arrived in The Uncertain World. Kushumai placed the still unconscious girl against the door.

'You will awaken in the Moving Hills,' murmured the Huntress. It's the door closest to Yadigar. You will be reunited with your friends, and Robin. Brave Amber, brave little Hamingja ...

Kushumai placed her hands on some of the Graphems carved into the door and chanted the words of a Galdr. There was a flash, and Amber vanished.

31

The Ravenous Desert

There was a movement at the window. Robin had been waiting, concealed in the dark, for more than two hours now, and he was beginning to wonder whether the boy in the jeweller's shop had been making fun of him. But then he caught sight of a hand waving in his direction from the small basement window with bars in front of it. Silently, he crept over and peered in. He could make out Kyle's face.

'I don't know who you are, but I know the medallion you showed my master, the jeweller. If you help me escape, I'll tell you everything I know.'

'I'm a Little Man of Virdu,' replied Robin after a moment's hesitation. 'But how do I know you'll keep your word? The minute you're free, you might run off.'

'If you're from Virdu, then I'm an Ork! As for my word, you have it, I swear. So?'

'OK then,' Robin said after deciding that he had nothing to lose. 'How do I get you out of there?'

'It's easy. One of the bars has been eaten away by rust. I can't break it on my own, but between the two of us ...'

Robin grabbed the bar and Kyle did the same on his side. They pulled and pushed hard until the iron bar suddenly gave way. Then Robin helped the young slave, whose ankles were still chained, to squeeze himself through the narrow opening.

'Thank you, whoever you are,' said the boy. Now, let's not waste any time. We've got to get out of this town fast.'

'And go where?'

'Into the Ravenous Desert.'

'The desert?' asked Robin in alarm.

'Unless you'd rather be hanged. That's what happens to anyone who helps a slave escape, in Ferghana.'

'Right, let's move!' agreed Robin. 'Let's look on the positive side. I didn't get a chance to perfect my tan this summer.'

Then they hurried towards the city walls with Kyle leaning heavily on Robin to walk. Soon they reached a gap, used in the past by robbers to slip into and out of the wealthy city unnoticed.

They got out of the city without mishap. The moon shone feebly, then disappeared altogether behind a cloud. Ferghana slept the heavy slumber of those who are just a little too sure of themselves. The secret gap in the wall had probably just escaped the notice of the sentries and was unguarded. The two boys headed due south into the desert, but their progress was hampered by the chains on Kyle's ankles which they had been unable to remove.

They walked as fast as they could until dawn, to place as great a distance as possible between themselves and the city of merchants.

'Whew!' gasped Kyle collapsing on the sand next to Robin when they eventually reached the desert. 'Right, now tell me who you really are.'

'I told you, a Little Man of Virdu,' replied Robin getting his breath back.

'Oh sure,' said Kyle sarcastically. 'For your information, the people of Virdu have deep voices, would rather die than run, and speak Ska a lot better than you.'

'Let's keep to our deal,' interrupted Robin curtly. 'I helped you, now it's your turn. What can you tell me about this medallion?'

Kyle stared long and hard at the apprentice sorcerer. He looked peevish and kept his mouth obstinately shut.

'OK,' sighed Robin, realizing he wasn't going to get anywhere. 'I'll come clean.'

He removed the thick hood of his Virdu cloak and revealed his face.

Kyle was flabbergasted. 'But you're a kid!'

'Like you,' retorted Robin, amused by Kyle's astonishment.

'I mean ... You ... but how?'

'That's the wrong question,' Robin corrected him. 'It's not how, but where, and why. Do you want to know?'

Kyle nodded vigorously, his eyes wide.

Robin went on. 'I am not from this world. I come from another place, called The Lost Isle. Yes, I'm a kid, well, up to a point. And I'm here ... because I'm a bit crazy! In any case, it would be really helpful to me if you could just tell me what you know about the medallion that I showed the jeweller. I've lost some friends and I'm trying to find them. And perhaps this medallion ...'

There was a silence.

Kyle avoided Robin's eye, then he began his story, 'My name's Kyle, as you know. About a year ago, bandits attacked my people, who live in the desert. They captured me and sold me in Ferghana, to the old man you saw in the shop.'

'That's terrible,' sympathised Robin.

'Oh! He never harmed me. He wasn't really wicked. It could have been worse. ...'

'What about ... the medallion?' broke in Robin, who wanted to get straight to the point.

'I was coming to that. The medallion is worn by the henchmen of Commander Thunku, the Master of Yadigar. I know, because my tribe is always moving around and sometimes travels through the Yadigar region.'

'Can you tell me more about this Thunku?' asked Robin.

'He's a violent man who is much feared. His bandits terrorize the whole region. He's head of an army made up of men, but also Orks and other monsters. He has many powerful friends. Like Lord Sha, for example.'

Robin shuddered. He'd heard that name before! Or rather, he'd read it somewhere. Maybe at Gifdu. Yes, that was it, at Gifdu, in a book about The Uncertain World! But what had it said? Robin couldn't remember.

'What else?' he pressed Kyle.

'Well, as far as I know, Thunku has never waged war on my people. We have an ancient bond as a result of a peace treaty signed a very long time ago. The desert belongs to the Men of the Sands, and the Stone Road belongs to the city!'

Robin thought about Kyle's words for a moment. He fished the map of The Uncertain World out of his bag. Ferghana was here, the Stone Road and Yadigar there; and they were here, in the desert. He sighed.

So much time had already passed since they had come through The Door! Were his friends having as much trouble as he was? And above all, would they be in Yadigar, as he had hoped from the beginning? Were they even still alive?

'What's that?' asked Kyle, curious to see what his new friend was looking at.

'It's a map of your world. You see, we're about here.'

Kyle seemed fascinated.

'Is it the first time you've seen a map?'

'Yes ... and those words, there, and there, what do they say?'

Robin looked where he was pointing. 'They're the names of places. Can't you read?'

'No.'

'Aren't there any schools where you come from?' asked Robin.

'There are, but not many. They're for the select few.'

'You don't know how lucky you are.. Come on, let's get moving,' said Robin, putting away the map. 'Oh! By the way,' he added, stretching his hand out to Kyle, 'I'm Robin.'

They set off again on their exhausting journey. A few hours later, the first light of dawn broke. Kyle grew agitated.

'We must find a Bokht, quickly, before the sun rises.'

'A Bokht?' asked Robin in surprise. His companion's panic was making him nervous.

'Yes, a slab of rock. ... We must find one quickly otherwise the Ravenous Desert, when it awakens, will gobble us up.'

Robin saved his questions until later and helped Kyle in his frantic search. Luckily, Kyle soon yelled triumphantly, 'Over there, I can see one!'

They rushed over to a large flat rock, as big as a boat, and clambered onto it. A few moments later, the sun appeared. Then the sand around them began to boil and quake. Beneath the big rock, they could feel the desert moving. Eventually everything became still. Robin looked inquiringly at his friend.

'The Ravenous Desert is alive,' explained Kyle to a puzzled Robin. 'During the day, it gobbles up anything that's not made of rock – living creatures, metal, wood, anything. But at night, it sleeps and you can cross it without fear. ...'

'And there are men who live in this burning hell?'

'Yes, the Men of the Sands. It's simply a matter of adapting.'

Then they fell silent, to save their saliva, as they hadn't brought any water with them.

32

A nasty encounter

'Right, and now where are we going?'

'Let me look at the map. ... Your friends dropped us around here. That road to the left must go to Ferghana. I think we should take it. After the Moving Hills, there must be a fork leading to Yadigar.'

Coral leaned over Romaric's shoulder and glanced at the map without interest. 'If you say so. But let's hurry up and move, I'm baking in this sun!'

The Sixth Tribe of the People of the Sea had set Coral and Romaric down on a stretch of coast abandoned by the Gommons, a good distance from the sinister territory of Yenibohor.

Matsi had sobbed broken-heartedly when Coral had hugged her. 'Don't let anyone push you around just because your father is only the Keeper of the Salvaged Objects. People will only value you if you value yourself,' she had told her.

Romaric shook Wal's hand warmly and thanked him

for his help. They waved goodbye to the rafts until they were out of sight, and then headed inland, where they'd been assured they would come across a road.

'There are already two of us now,' said Romaric picking his way among the ruts caused by the wheels of countless carts. 'It won't be long until we're all together again! We just need to get to Yadigar. Didn't you say that Thomas's medallion seemed like the best lead to follow?'

'Yes, that was the first thing that occurred to me. You know, I've always had a weakness for jewellery!'

Romaric looked at her in amazement. Coral was laughing at herself without a prompt from anyone else!

'Yes, but seriously,' he went on, fiddling with the map he was still holding, 'that medallion is the only clue that we all have. I thought of it immediately too. We just have to hope the others did the same.'

They continued for a while in silence. Romaric, unusually quiet, seemed preoccupied and agitated. Suddenly, he burst out, 'Coral, I ... I haven't really thanked you for saving my life the other day with the jellyfish. ... What you did was incredibly brave. I don't know if I'd have been able to do the same. In any case, I'll never forget it.'

Coral blushed slightly and shot her friend a look of gratitude.

'I'm sure you'd have done exactly the same in my place. But I don't think I'd ever be able to do it again.'

'Really? Why not?'

'I'm petrified of jellyfish! Absolutely petrified!'

'And you still dived in?'

Romaric was stunned. Her bravery took on a whole new dimension.

Flattered, Coral basked in her friend's admiration. But she couldn't help remarking mischievously, 'I absolutely had to show you my new earrings! And as you were so slow getting on board the raft ...'

'You really are astonishing!'

'Thank you!' said Coral with a wink.

Eventually, at nightfall, they reached the foot of the Moving Hills.

Romaric lit a little fire of dried grasses and they sat around it to eat the smoked fish Wal had given them on parting. Then they snuggled up together in their Virdu cloaks, but the future Knight of the Wind had difficulty getting to sleep.

*

At lunchtime the next day, they reached the fork Romaric had been anticipating. One of the roads headed due south. They set off down it.

'If all goes well, we should be within sight of Yadigar tomorrow,' announced Romaric.

'I wonder what the city is like?'

'According to Wal, it's not very nice. He says it's the meeting place for all the scum of The Uncertain World.'

'Lovely! To think that right now I could have been at home, on the terrace, sipping an iced tea,' sighed Coral.

The path wound through rocky gorges hemmed in by steep hills, and followed the bed of a long dried-up stream. There were no trees and no plants. They were enveloped in silence.

'This place makes my flesh creep!' confessed Coral glancing anxiously about her. 'Let's get out of here as fast as we can.'

They hurried along the path.

Suddenly, a long whistle filled the narrow gorge. Two men leaped out in front of them and blocked their way, brandishing weapons. Bandits! The first, a short, deformed character with one bulging eye and a thread of saliva dribbling from his gaping, toothless mouth, made a rush for the terrified Coral, waving his flail around like a maniac. The second, who was very tall and dressed in a bearskin, held his spear under their noses.

They were prisoners. Romaric clenched his fists but, unarmed, there was no point in putting up a fight. He let them tie his hands and chain his feet, as they had already done to Coral.

The bandits took a track that climbed upwards, perpendicular to the main path. The dwarf led the way and his foul-smelling companion brought up the rear.

They came to a cave, whose entrance was partially concealed by a huge rock. Their captors pushed them inside. At the back of the cave were stacks of padlocked chests. On a makeshift bed lay a stocky man who was coughing and spitting blood which spattered his dark, bushy beard.

The two bandits led Coral and Romaric to him.

'Bah! Kids. ... Have they got any stones?'

'Not many, chief,' replied the bandit in the bearskin. 'We searched them and this is all we found. ...'

He deposited a small handful of precious stones, a

gold necklace, a silver bracelet and two blue earrings on his chief's bed.

'It's better than nothing,' grunted the bandit whose hairy chest was covered in filthy bandages. He'd obviously been wounded during a recent ambush. 'We'll decide what to do with them tomorrow. Thunku pays as much for girls as he does for boys, and he pays well.'

The dwarf sniggered, which made both Romaric and Coral shudder.

Then, without further ado, the two friends were led to the back of the cave where they were bound hand and foot.

'Oh, this is awful!' cried Coral whose chin was trembling.

'It'll be all right,' Romaric tried to comfort her. 'We'll get out of here, I promise you.'

Two more bandits arrived in the sheltered cave, which brought the total number of gaolers to five, including their bedridden leader. Romaric sighed. Five were too many to take on. He was trying to come up with an escape plan, but everything he thought of seemed hopeless. Perhaps under cover of dark ...

A young archer who was painfully thin and whose face was split down the middle by a hideous scar, burst into the cave. Breathless, he announced the arrival of travellers at the entrance to the gorge.

'Right, everyone in position,' ordered the bandit chief. 'We'll hold up this lot and tomorrow we clear out of here. There are enough stones in these chests for us all to live like kings!'

His declaration was greeted by shouts of joy. The bandits all rushed out. Romaric seized the opportunity to try and loosen his bonds. But they had been tied up by men who knew what they were doing, and all he achieved was to chafe his wrists.

Beside him, Coral stirred. 'You know, I'm much happier knowing that horrid dwarf is away from the cave,' she whispered. 'Did you see how he was looking at us? I've still got goose bumps!'

'Try and keep calm,' replied Romaric. 'I'm here. We'll get through this together ... somehow.'

33

The bandits get a nasty surprise

'This place is spooky.'

'It is indeed, my musician friend.'

The giant with the tattooed skull gazed about him with his grey eyes. He didn't like the look of the gorge they had just entered. If he himself wanted to ambush travellers to rob or murder them, this was definitely the place he would choose!

'Do you think we're in danger?' asked Godfrey nervously fiddling with the strings of his zither.

'That's my problem! We have a deal, you entertain me with your songs in the evenings, and I handle perils on the journey, right?' The giant from the steppes gave a little laugh.

Godfrey ran his hand through his hair.

It was true that since they'd parted company with the merchants from Ferghana, nobody had given them any trouble. And no wonder. Looking at Tofann, nobody would want to get on the wrong side of him!

Suddenly, a long whistle echoed through the gorge. Before it had died away the giant had vanished, and Godfrey was left alone to confront the men who leaped out from behind the rocks.

They looked at each other anxiously. 'Weren't there two of them, eh, archer?'

'I definitely saw two of 'em at the entrance to the gorge,' said the young bandit defensively.

'If you saw two,' said a one-armed robber brandishing a hatchet in his good hand, 'where's the other one then?'

'He's right here!'

Tofann appeared out of nowhere. He grabbed the one-armed robber's skull and hit it against the metal breastplate of the leather tunic that protected his heart. Quick as a flash, he pulled a knife out of his boot and plunged it into the man's chest. The robber toppled backwards, smashing his shield on a rock as he fell.

The others were numb with shock.

The giant had pulled an impressive sword out of the metal scabbard on his back. 'Now let's get down to business!'

He made a swift scything movement with it, nearly decapitating the archer, who skilfully ducked just in time. Another stroke almost cut the bandit in the bearskin in half. He groaned in pain before collapsing dead on the ground. The archer, abandoning his bow, had unsheathed a dagger and stood bravely confronting Tofann. The giant was nimble on his feet, and his movements were swift and precise. The archer had great difficulty avoiding the blows raining down from his formidable opponent. But he bravely attempted a few thrusts, which Tofann easily parried. Finally, the giant wounded the young man's hand, forcing him to drop his dagger. Then, he stabbed him in the thigh, watching him keel over in pain. Lying on the ground, the archer glowered at Tofann, who looked him up and down, his sword resting casually on the archer's shoulder. The contrast between the extreme thinness of the archer and the powerful frame of the giant was remarkable, to say the least. 'Don't worry, kid. I don't hit a man when he's down. Especially when he's put up a good fight. You're not going to die.'

At the start of the battle, Godfrey had found refuge behind a rock and watched the fight in horror. With the young archer out of action, the only bandit left to face the warrior was the disfigured dwarf, who stared at Tofann with an expression of indescribable terror on his face.

Tofann advanced towards him. The gnome flung down his flail and fled shrieking. The giant warrior set off in pursuit, followed closely by Godfrey, who had no intention of being left alone with the archer and the dead bodies.

Breathless, Godfrey entered a cave lit by torches. Tofann had cornered the fugitive and knocked him unconscious. Now, he was bellowing furiously as he bound and gagged a man who was lying on a bed.

'Godfrey! Oh, wow! It's Godfrey!'

Godfrey swung round and peered towards the back of the cave. Tied up against some chests, Romaric and Coral were staring at him as if he were a ghost.

ᥱ

'This is where we part company,' Tofann announced to the three friends.

The giant had insisted on accompanying them to the mouth of the gorge. Vultures were already circling hungrily above the site of the battle.

The archer, who had apparently been only lightly wounded, had vanished.

'Are you sure you won't change your mind?' asked Godfrey for the umpteenth time. He was distraught at the idea of losing his friend.

Tofann laughed and pointed to the huge bag that now hung over his shoulder. 'Why should I fight for anyone else now I'm rich enough to do it for fun?'

As soon as Tofann and Godfrey had freed the two prisoners, they had opened the chests to reveal a treasure trove of precious stones and jewels. Godfrey, Romaric and Coral had refused to touch the loot that had cost the lives of so many people, but Tofann had stuffed the treasure into his bag and then sealed the entrance to the cave with big rocks.

'Just follow the road. It leads straight to Yadigar.'

'Suppose we meet more bandits?' suggested Godfrey, reasonably, he thought.

'That's your problem, now,' replied the giant in a gentler tone. 'You won't have someone to watch over you for ever!'

Seeing how upset Godfrey was, Coral realized it was best not to linger over the goodbyes. She stepped forward, stood on tiptoe and kissed the giant on the cheek. 'Thank you again for saving us,' she said simply.

Romaric gave Tofann a look filled with respect and admiration, held out his hand, and tried not to wince when the giant shook it. Tofann was a warrior through and through, a supreme fighter. Perhaps he could be like him someday, not quite so big and wild, perhaps. More the strong and noble variety!

Lastly, the battle-scarred giant embraced Godfrey in an affectionate bear hug. The boy found it hard not to cry. He had grown terribly fond of this calm, good-humoured man who was so strong and fierce yet so sensitive with his friends. Brave as he was, Godfrey really didn't want to part company with his comforting presence.

Tofann gently detached himself from Godfrey's hug and walked off into the distance, waving until he was out of sight.

'Come and visit me in the steppes, if you ever get lost in the north!' he called out.

The three friends looked at each other. 'Right, well ... umm, we've got business to attend to, haven't we?' ventured Godfrey timidly.

'You bet we have!' said Romaric, clapping his friend on the back.

'Forward march, my friends!' urged Coral, delighted to see that, despite their ordeal, they hadn't lost heart.

Arm in arm, the three friends set off for Yadigar.

34

The Men of the Sands

The sun was blazing down. The two boys, trapped on the Bokht – the big slab of rock protecting them from the Ravenous Desert – were beginning to feel desperately thirsty. Robin had taken the spare Virdu cloak out of his rucksack and given it to Kyle to shield him from the scorching rays. Kyle sat very still, clasping his knees, his head resting on his arms.

Robin stood scanning the horizon, his hands shading his eyes from the harsh glare. 'Visitors!' he cried suddenly. 'People, over there, coming towards us!'

Kyle leaped up and looked where Robin was pointing. His friend was right, a group of men dressed in blue and carrying long rifles was heading straight towards them.

'Now we've had it,' moaned Robin. 'I bet they're soldiers from Ferghana sent to catch us.'

Kyle said nothing.

'Oh no, and we can't even move from this rock. We're cornered! And you think it's funny?' fumed Robin, pacing up and down, while Kyle just sat smiling.

'At least we'll get a drink of water soon,' Kyle replied calmly.

'Oh great!' said Robin. 'Even the thought of a drink of water doesn't exactly fill me with joy, if we're rotting in a prison cell waiting to be hanged.'

The blue men were making slow progress. Then Robin noticed their curious footwear. Their feet were strapped to large, flat stones which they cleverly used like snowshoes, and they held batons with round pebbles on the ends.

'So that's how they do it!' he said, striking his forehead. 'To think I was planning to jump off the Bokht and take my chances on the sand.'

'That would have been a fatal mistake,' said Kyle grinning. He seemed to find the whole situation very amusing. 'Only the Men of the Sands have a way of moving around in broad daylight without being eaten by the desert.'

'So they aren't they merchants from Ferghana?' asked Robin in surprise.

'Merchants? In the Ravenous Desert, in the middle of the day? No, trust me, they are Men of the Sands. From the Blue Tribe, actually.'

Suddenly a great excitement seemed to take hold of the curiously shod group. They started pointing at the boys, shouting, and waving their rifles around.

'Are they going to hurt us?' asked Robin anxiously.

'I really don't think so,' smiled Kyle.

Kyle was right. The little group of Men of the Sands,

who had now drawn close, were noisily expressing their delight at having found them. They crowded excitedly around Robin and the young slave boy. Robin couldn't understand what all the fuss was about, but he soon noticed the respect these men showed Kyle. First, they gave the boys some slightly salty water to drink. Then Robin was hoisted onto the shoulders of the sturdiest of their rescuers, and Kyle, because of his chains, was carried in another's arms. The group set off again and the Bokht, on which they had been marooned, was soon a speck in the desert.

'I didn't get round to telling you,' explained Kyle in answer to Robin's unspoken question, 'but I am the son of the tribal chiefs of the Men of the Sands!'

'How come, the son of the *chiefs*?'

'When I was a baby,' explained Kyle, 'I was found beside a well. Water is sacred for my people. So the Men of the Sands decided it was the gods who had entrusted me to their care and, to honour them, they asked their chiefs to take care of me. ... And that's how I became the son of the chiefs of the three tribes that make up my people!'

'So that means you don't know who your real parents are?' asked Robin.

Kyle's face clouded over. He replied in a flat voice, 'No.'

'Well, we've got something in common there,' said Robin in an attempt to sound reassuring. 'Well, sort of. I've never met my father ...'

This painful thought silenced Robin. He could

suddenly picture his mother's smiling face, and it made him feel as if everything he loved, his whole life, was light years away from this desert. ...

But his thoughts were interrupted by his bearer complaining that his shifting about was causing him to lose his balance, and he was brought firmly back to reality.

A few hours later, they reached a big camp with lots of tents spread over a huge Bokht in the centre of a valley.

Their appearance caused a tremendous commotion.

'Am I glad we've arrived?' groaned Robin with relief. 'I'm feeling quite travel sick from being bumped around.'

'Are you all right?' asked Kyle cheerfully. 'You've gone very green!'

'And your eye will be very black in a minute if you don't stop making fun of me!'

'Instead of complaining, think about the poor man who had to carry you on his shoulders!'

While they teased each other playfully, happy their ordeal was over, people had gathered around them. A very tall, thin man, dressed in blue robes like the others, stepped forward, took Kyle in his arms and hugged him tight.

The boy murmured a few words in his ear and the man turned towards Robin. 'You helped my son escape. My tribe is your tribe.'

He had spoken in Ska, in a steady, grave tone. Robin guessed that he must be one of the three chiefs of the Men of the Sands, and therefore one of Kyle's three fathers. Soon, men, women and children were crowding round him and congratulating him. He was led to one of the big hut-like tents, where he was seated and plied with food and drink.

After a while, Kyle joined him. His chains had been removed and he wore the dark blue robes of the Men of the Sands, except his were also adorned with blood-red and white sashes.

'The three tribes are mine,' explained the boy who looked quite regal in his new attire. 'It's natural that I should honour them all by wearing their colours.'

'You look very grand, Kyle. What happens to us now?'

'Well,' said Kyle, who seemed lost in a dream, 'this evening the tribe is holding a celebration in your honour.'

'That's wonderful. But ... tomorrow, will someone be able to get me back on the road to Yadigar? I don't want to be a spoilsport, but the days are passing by and I don't have much time left.'

'I'll take you there myself,' Kyle reassured him. 'But I don't know if it's such a good idea. Yadigar's a pretty rough place.'

'Maybe it's not such a good idea,' avowed Robin, 'but it's the only one I have.'

'We'll see about that tomorrow,' replied Kyle. 'For now, let's just enjoy ourselves.'

Robin agreed, and soon his spirits had lifted.

❧

'What do your people do for a living?' Robin asked Kyle, who was sitting beside him on one of the little goatskin-covered wooden stools around a big, low table heaped with food and drinks.

It was a dark, moonless night, and the celebrations, which had spilled off the Bokht onto the sleeping desert, were in full swing. Nearby, cheered on by the crowd, a man was coaxing exquisite notes from a black metal flute, while girls were performing exotic desert dances.

'My people live mainly from trading Gambouris – purple flower-shaped crystals you find in the desert sand,' replied Kyle after a moment's pause. That enables us to buy what we need to survive and continue our nomadic existence, wandering from Bokht to Bokht, from waterhole to waterhole.'

'I envy you,' sighed Robin. 'You seem so happy.'

'It hasn't always been like this, you know,' went on Kyle. 'Legend has it that long, long ago, our tribes belonged to a people that used to travel from one world to another, just as we do from well to well. One day, the three tribes – which in those days were one – happened to be in The Uncertain World. The Smuggler, who knew how to get people from one world to the other, died suddenly, taking his secret with him. And ever since, we've been condemned to live in this dangerous desert.'

'It's a great story,' enthused Robin. 'But is it just a story or is it what really happened?'

'Nobody knows. But we have preserved something from those ancient times – the Ceremony of the Dead Moon. You'll see later, it's nearly time. The cycle has begun.'

The two boys chatted on for a while. Eventually, the flute fell silent and the singing and laughing stopped.

The chief called on all the members of the tribe to rise

and gather under the star-studded sky. They all held hands. At their head, the chief's tall and graceful form adopted different positions, which the others all imitated. The human chain seemed to take on a life of its own, like a snake. Then the man began chanting, using words whose meaning had long since been forgotten, just as Kyle had described. The strange ritual lasted for about ten minutes, then everybody returned to their activities and the festivities resumed.

'It's our way of preserving our distant past,' explained Kyle sitting back down on the stool.

But Robin was no longer listening. He had opened his black leather covered notebook, and was feverishly scribbling everything he had seen and heard during the ceremony.

35

Yadigar

Early the next morning, still bleary-eyed, Robin clambered onto the shoulders of a desert-walker and set off, escorted by a few men from the Blue Tribe and by Kyle, who, like the others, wore stone sandshoes.

'Aaagh!' winced Robin who soon felt sick again from the swaying motion.

'You shouldn't have drunk so much sour-apple cider, yesterday,' taunted Kyle.

'Leave me alone!' said Robin, winking at his friend.

They trudged on for a several hours. It took great skill to walk wearing the stone sandshoes, but the Men of the Sands were swift, wading across the moving sand amazingly fast. At last, they reached the Stone Road, which was built of giant paving stones, and here Robin got his first glimpse of Yadigar.

'This is it,' announced Kyle. 'We're going to drop you here. We can't go any further. Remember, I told you, the Men of the Sands have a pact with the priests of Yadigar;

the Ravenous Desert's ours while everything that lies beyond, including the Stone Road, belongs to the City of Fir.'

Robin slid down from his improvized mount and went over to his friend. 'Kyle, thank you, thank you for everything.'

'Thank *you*!' replied the Son of the Chiefs with a radiant smile. 'You're the one who freed me, remember.'

They hugged each other awkwardly.

'You can always rely on me,' added Kyle becoming serious. 'Always, for anything.'

'Thank you for your friendship,' said Robin in a choked voice. 'Will we see each other again?'

'Perhaps. Who knows?'

'I really hope we do, Kyle.'

From one of the men's bags, Kyle took out the Virdu cloak Robin had given him, on the Bokht, to protect him from the sun.

'Here, this is yours, take it. A Virdu cloak, that's valuable.'

'Keep it, Kyle. Then you'll think of me every time you wear it.'

Kyle grinned from ear to ear. Robin found it hard to tear himself away from his new-found friend and the Men of the Sands. But Yadigar was his only chance of finding his friends from The Lost Isle. He sighed and drew the hood of his own cloak over his head, then stepped onto the road that looked as if it had appeared from nowhere in the midst of the sands. He waved goodbye to the blue men who were heading back into the desert, and shot Kyle one last parting look.

Robin wasn't the only person making his way to Yadigar. Gangs of Orks and men-at-arms walked alongside merchants with carts piled high. The road became increasingly crowded as they neared the city. The merchants would no doubt trade their wares for the spoils of Thunku's looting, which they would sell in Ferghana or elsewhere.

Robin tried to appear unobtrusive and withdrew into his voluminous grey cloak.

Walking towards the massive gate, the only entrance to Yadigar, he gazed upwards, and there, perched above, was the statue of the huge lion surrounded by flames, the same as the image on the Ork's medallion. Then, just as he was about to go through into the fortified city, he was stopped by a guard. He looked just like the one who had nearly captured him at the entrance to Ferghana – human in appearance but actually a cross between a man and an Ork.

'Hey, you there! Little Man of Virdu. Come with me!'

Robin froze, scared out of his wits. He eventually regained his composure and replied in his deepest voice, 'What's the problem?'

'Don't mess with me, midget! You know very well that Lord Thunku has banned your people from the town. Come on, this way.'

'Listen, there must be some way we can sort this out ...' ventured Robin.

He wasn't able to say another word, for the Hybrid guard had whisked out his big serrated sword from its sheath and was holding it to his throat. 'OK, OK, I'll follow you!'

The guard, his sword at the ready, propelled Robin through the streets of Yadigar in the direction of a big building that dominated the city.

Yadigar was as spread out as Ferghana, its twin sister, but was different in most other ways. On the outer walls, which were in perfect repair, guards armed to the hilt kept a constant watch; no slave would have the remotest chance of escaping from this place! The city was swarming with fighters – mercenaries come to offer their services to the Master of the City. Scuffles broke out frequently among them, in the streets and in the many taverns where they hung out to pass the time. Robin took all this in and it made him nervous. He was almost glad to be escorted by the monster who had arrested him. No fire-eaters, bogus magicians or jewellers in Yadigar; the city was devoted to violence and war, and the only trade going on was that of weapons and plunder!

Eventually, they came to an imposing building. The visible part, which towered several storeys above them, exuding luxury and splendour, was like a glamorous oriental palace. But it had a hidden, underground section, where Robin was taken, that extended down several levels and was like a grim catacomb.

A heavy iron door swung open and Robin was pushed down a dank corridor until he reached a cell with heavy iron bars. He was thrown inside.

36

Prisoners!

Once Robin's eyes had grown used to the dark, he became aware that he was in a huge, vaulted room. First his gaze registered the barred door, then the thick walls glistening with damp and patches of stinking black mould.

He soon realized that there was absolutely no means of escape. Worse, he sensed he wasn't alone in the cell. Towards the far wall, standing or sprawled on wooden benches were clustered several people who were staring silently at the new arrival.

'I told you we'd all meet up in Yadigar!' came a delighted shout.

With a shock, Robin recognized Romaric's voice. And there was his cousin, coming towards him followed by three other equally familiar shapes.

'Romaric! Godfrey! Coral! Amber!' Hooting with joy, he fell into their arms.

'Oh, thank goodness! It's wonderful that you survived!'

'Miraculous more like,' grunted Amber after hugging Robin hard. 'So what went wrong when we came through The Door?'

'I can explain. ... The main thing is that you're all safe and sound!'

'Only just,' protested Godfrey raising his hand. 'You won't believe where I landed! At the top of a huge tower that—'

'What about me?' broke in Coral, her hands on her hips. 'Do you think it was fun being on a rotten raft surrounded by yucky jellyfish?'

'*Surrounded by yucky jellyfish!*' mimicked Godfrey, laughing affectionately.

'Can I—' ventured Romaric.

'And we were captured by bandits. That was no joke,' butted in Coral, interrupting Romaric.

'Yes, and while we're talking about bandits, if I hadn't been there—'

'If you hadn't been there? Cheek! It was Tofann who saved us, not you, Godfrey. Mind you, if you'd started playing your zither, maybe ...'

'Shut up, all of you!' yelled Robin to make himself heard. 'We've obviously all got loads to tell each other.'

'Yeah,' said Amber. 'The others have, but not me. Nothing happened to me, other than really awful headaches.'

'We've got a headache too, from listening to you worrying about what you can't remember!' teased Romaric.

'I'll give you a headache!' threatened Amber advancing towards him.

'Hey, you lot! Do something!' shrieked Romaric as Amber grabbed his neck.

Robin rushed over and pretended to separate them. It was so wonderful to be together again. Just then, he noticed a boy dressed in brightly coloured clothes, standing shyly to one side.

'I forgot,' said Romaric who'd noticed his glance, 'this is Toti. He's been clinging to us ever since we arrived here. The others are all grown-ups, and they're not particularly nice.'

'He's a very sweet boy,' added Coral.

'No one said he wasn't,' sighed Amber. 'But we don't stare at him all the time like you do.'

'It's his clothes. Toti's got something you don't have, and that's class,' retorted Coral, in Ska.

'Oh, thank you,' replied Toti rather embarrassed, more by Romaric and Godfrey's mocking grins than by Coral's remark.

'Why are you here?' Robin asked him.

'I was a servant, a page, in Lord Thunku's palace. I was hungry and I stole an apple. I got caught,' he replied matter-of-factly.

'That's terrible!' exclaimed Robin.

'Oh, I'm lucky. ... A lot of prisoners don't even know why they're here.'

'Do you know what's going to happen to us?' asked Romaric.

'No. I imagine the chief officer will come and see you when he has time, or when he feels like it.'

'Charming!' said Amber. 'And in the meantime?'

'We could start by telling each other about our adventures,' suggested Robin.

'Good idea!' agreed Coral. 'Come on, let's sit down.'

Robin, Amber and Coral found a corner at the back of the cell where they were joined by Toti, Godfrey and Romaric, all chatting nineteen to the dozen.

'... When the three of us arrived in Yadigar after the incident in the gorge,' said Godfrey coming to the end of his story, 'we were sorry we hadn't listened to Tofann! Although we did follow his advice and get rid of our Virdu cloaks. ...'

'It was good advice too!' said Robin. 'The Little Men aren't exactly welcome in Yadigar!'

'Yes,' went on Godfrey, 'but Tofann also suggested we bring with us a few precious stones from the bandits' hoard, and that we didn't do. We didn't want to become thieves like them. Result: at the gate, we weren't able to pay the entrance fee, and we ended up in jail like common criminals!'

'It's enough to put you off being honest,' grumbled Romaric.

'Your turn, Amber,' ordered Robin.

'Well, honestly, nothing much happened to me,' confessed Amber sounding disappointed. 'I found myself alone, lying in the grass next to a door. I felt very weak. My legs were like jelly. I remember thinking that it wasn't easy going from one world to another!'

'Can you describe the place where the door stood?' Robin asked her.

'It was in the bottom of a valley. All around there were grassy hills, as far as the eye could see. I took out my map of The Uncertain World, and I said to myself that I was probably in the Moving Hills.

'That's weird,' said Robin, puzzled. 'I arrived by that door too, but you weren't there, I'm sure of it!'

'No, you weren't there either. I thought, I'm all alone, there's something wrong, Robin's messed up again! The worse thing was that I had this terrible headache. I think I'd been asleep for a very long time. I remember dreaming of horses, and a long ride. Then, when I was able to stand, I wandered for hours until I met a caravan of merchants. They captured me and tied me up. I was helpless and completely exhausted. And that's not like me at all.'

'True!' chorused Romaric and Robin.

'Then,' went on Amber with a shrug, 'they bundled me into a wagon. I heard the driver say to someone else that I was going to be sold as a slave to this Lord Thunku, in Yadigar, who would pay a high price for me. I didn't care! All I wanted was to go to sleep. And that's what I did until they dumped me here.'

'OK, let's see what we have,' suggested Robin after a long silence. 'Godfrey, you landed in an abandoned city, on top of a mysterious tower, filled with books and sorcerer's instruments. ... Well done for escaping, by the way!'

'Fear lent me wings,' replied Godfrey modestly. 'Now, I know what you went through when you ran away from Gifdu!'

'Yeah, too right. ... Anything else, Godfrey?' continued Robin.

'No. Other than that the name of the abandoned city is Jaghatel, according to the map of The Uncertain World. And that I immediately had a bad feeling about that tower. A premonition that helped me find the courage to escape.'

'And you, Coral,' Robin went on, 'you ended up on a raft belonging to the People of the Sea. Romaric joined you there later.'

'Yes, I just dropped in,' shrugged Romaric grinning.

'Coral has told us everything she knows about these People of the Sea. Romaric, you said something about priests, too?'

'The priests of Yenibohor. Everyone in The Uncertain World seems to fear them,' Romaric explained.

'Fear and hate them,' said Coral. 'Apparently they're involved in child kidnappings.'

'Well if Agatha's been captured by the priests of Yenibohor, we've got our work cut out,' sighed Godfrey.

'Isn't that very unlikely?' interrupted Robin. 'The Ork's medallion is directly linked to Yadigar.'

'What about me?' asked Amber who was frustrated at having nothing of interest to tell her friends. 'Why am I the only one to have fallen into a deep sleep and woken up with a nasty headache?'

'That's certainly a mystery,' agreed Robin. 'It's also odd how you arrived through the same door as me but clearly not at the same time, otherwise we'd have seen each other.'

'I can explain the headache. It's all the nagging. ...' teased Godfrey.

'Stop it, this is no time for fighting!' said Romaric trying to smooth things over as Amber started pulling Godfrey's shirt up over his head.

'Ssh! Calm down!' broke in Toti who'd been left out of the conversation as the friends had been talking in the language of The Lost Isle. 'The chief officer's coming!'

The grating of locks being drawn back and the light of torch at the other end of the corridor confirmed Toti's warning. They all held their breath.

37

Commander Thunku

A guard opened the door of their cell. He was flanked by two men. No doubt, the well-fed, smug-looking one wearing expensive clothes was the prison chief. His companion didn't look like a soldier either – he had a shaven head and eagle eyes and wore a white robe that gave him the appearance of a sinister monk.

He spoke to the teenagers, pointing at them with a dry, bony hand which, Amber noticed, was missing a finger. 'You lot! Follow me.'

None of them moved; they were all waiting for Robin to decide what to do.

'Did you hear me?' bawled the guard, striking the bars with handle of his flail. Obey the orders of His Excellency Commander Thunku's Councillor!'

Robin sighed and, with the others behind him, followed the shaven-headed man out of the gaol.

'Farewell, prince of thieves,' whispered Coral theatrically to Toti, as they filed past him.

Robin and Godfrey shook his hand, Romaric gave him a friendly clap on the shoulder, and Amber murmured: 'Be strong!' as much to herself as to the page boy.

Then they followed the Councillor, the officer and the guard through a maze of endless corridors.

'Prince of thieves ... That was a bit over the top, wasn't it?' hissed Amber to her sister.

'It's funny,' added Romaric, 'I thought our little page looked rather relieved to see the back of us!'

'Don't be ridiculous!' retorted Coral.

Meanwhile, Godfrey was puzzled. He was convinced he'd seen the man with the beady eyes somewhere before ... He cast around in his mind, then gave up, shaking his head. He couldn't have, for he had never been to Yadigar before.

Finally, they came up into the daylight and were led into a vast hall at the heart of the palace.

'So these are the spies unmasked by my very perspicacious Councillor!' sneered Thunku, the Ruler of Yadigar, from the depths of a huge, carved wooden throne.

Commander Thunku was a mighty figure, whose face and hairy arms bore the scars of many battles. Meeting him for the first time, anyone could see that it wasn't out of love that his men obeyed him, and that he would probably beat the brains out of anyone who didn't do as he was told. His arrogance was formidable, and his voice boomed like thunder.

'Suppose you tell me what brings you here?' continued the Commander, whose beady black eyes flashed as he glared at the gang.

Their hearts sank. They said nothing. Coral shivered under the brute's gaze and, like the others, waited for Robin to speak first. Meanwhile, the apprentice sorcerer was desperately trying to think of a way out of their predicament.

'Oh dear, too shy too speak, are we? I'd hate to have to put you in the expert hands of my Councillor. Do you know what he used to do? He tortured heretics in Yenibohor!'

Stories about the priests of Yenibohor were fresh in the friends' minds, and they couldn't help glancing anxiously at the man standing discreetly to one side of the throne. Robin took a deep breath and addressed Thunku.

'Actually, we're members of the Blue Tribe of the Men of the Sands. We came here, against the advice of our chief, to buy some new weapons.'

Thunku sniggered and shook his head. 'Are you the leader? What is your name?'

'My name is ... Elyk.'

'Well, Elyk, I don't believe a word of your story.'

The Commander's voice took on a hard edge. 'I've even got an inkling about who you really are beneath your absurd disguises, and I think I know what you're looking for, despite your ridiculous explanations. Do you think children from The Uncertain World would dare set foot in Yadigar? How many kids have you seen in my city? Then he turned to the sentries by the door and commanded: 'Bring me the girl! Now!'

A few seconds later, two men returned, leading on a

rope a dark-haired girl who had purple rings under her eyes from crying. When she walked into the courtroom and caught sight of Robin, she froze. 'Robin?' she cried. 'Robin, is it you? But ... how?'

Standing in front of them, pale, thin and exhausted, was Agatha Balangru.

'You moron,' mumbled Amber under her breath; 'now, we've had it.'

From his throne, Thunku let out a roar of triumph. 'Well, Elyk, or should I call you Robin? Do you still maintain your ridiculous story? It's so touching, a gang of kids coming all the way from the world of The Lost Isle to rescue this worthless creature!'

He roared all the louder.

'You know what? When my Gommon brought this girl back from your world instead of the boy with extraordinary powers, my Lord nearly burst a blood vessel with rage. But he's more than made me pay for my mistake, because he left her with me! I've tried to make her into a decent servant, but she can't polish armour or even boil an egg. Who'd want her?'

He turned his gaze on Agatha who bit her lip, as hurt by the Commander's words as by Amber's smirk. Then he stared at Robin intrigued.

'About twelve years old, green eyes, seems smarter than the others. ... Have I found him at last? You see my boy, I think I'm going to make someone very happy. Someone who's been searching for you for a long time. And that makes two happy people, because before I hand you over to him, I'm going to demand a high price! I want to be allowed to move my men from one world to the other, not when he says so, but when I want to, for a bit of variety when we go looting!'

Suddenly there was a deafening bang, like an explosion. There were shouts and the sounds of battle. Then the door to the room smashed to smithereens. Pursued by men and armed Orks, a tall man whose clothes were covered in dust burst into the room.

Robin's blood ran cold. 'Master Quadehar!' he cried.

'Azhdar the Demon,' gasped Thunku.

38

Robin is angry

'Robin, are you all right?' asked Quadehar who had raced over to his apprentice at the foot of the throne. He kept the soldiers at bay by threatening them with the sorcerer's stance.

'Yes, Master! Am I happy to see you!'

'So am I, my boy. So am I. Thank the Gods of the Three Worlds that Thomas followed your instructions to the letter. And that the week's delay you insisted on expired the day before yesterday.'

Ready to fight off the sorcerer's attack, the guards released Agatha and the others, who ran to gather around Quadehar.

Behind them, Thunku had risen from his throne. He was seething with rage. 'Cursed demon! You dare to defy me in my own palace. I'll make you sorry for this!'

With a roar, Thunku leaped off the dais onto Quadehar, who, taken by surprise, didn't have the time to respond with a magic spell. The two men rolled to the ground. The sorcerer protected himself as best he could from the blows raining down on him. But Thunku was too strong.

With their enemy lying helpless on the ground, the Orks and the guards rushed jubilantly forward.

'Run!' yelled Quadehar.

'Catch them!' bellowed Thunku, who had pinned down the sorcerer in a powerful hold.

The Orks sprang towards the group of friends.

'Do something, Robin!' entreated Romaric.

'Yes, quick, please,' urged Coral wringing her hands. 'I don't fancy spending the rest of my life here as a slave, sweeping the floor and polishing armour.'

Robin took a deep breath and closed his eyes. He had to act. After the mishap in Ferghana, he had sworn he would leave the Graphems alone. Now, he had no choice. Reluctantly, he called them up. Just like when he was under the wagon of the bogus magician, not one of them appeared spontaneously. What was he to do? Beside him, Godfrey screamed as an Ork grabbed his arm.

'Do something, please,' begged Romaric, dodging a violent sword thrust.

Behind him, Robin could hear Quadehar moaning in pain. He felt a tremendous surge of anger well up inside him. With a superhuman effort of will, he forced the Graphems to line up in his mind. Two things were confirmed. First of all, the Graphems weren't their usual shapes, they were so distorted that he had trouble recognizing them. Secondly, as before, Thursaz was trying to stay in the background.

'You're the one I want, my friend,' murmured Robin between gritted teeth. 'Come, I'm calling you. Don't defy me. And there's no point sending Isaz instead!'

'What did you say?' asked Amber, who had stayed glued to his side since the start of the brawl and who was now fending off an Ork with a spear she'd picked up from the floor.

But Robin wasn't listening to her. His eyes still shut, he had managed to mobilize Thursaz. Abnormally swollen, the Graphem flickered like the flame of a dying candle.

Just as Coral, imprisoned in the arms of a repulsive Hybrid, shrieked, he invoked the Graphem. 'THUUUR-SAAAAZ!'

Everybody suddenly froze. In the bowels of the earth, a terrible rumbling began. The guards turned pale and dropped their swords, the Orks abandoned their prisoners and fled. Thunku himself released his grip and, pausing only to dart an astonished glance in Robin's direction and brandish his fist at Quadehar, he took to his heels and bolted.

'Quick, children,' said the sorcerer, getting to his feet with Romaric's help, 'we must get out of here.'

'What's happening? What have I done?' asked a horrified Robin.

'You cast a spell which, normally, at best is able to stop a Gommon in his tracks. But invoked by you, here, in The Uncertain World, it has shattered the nexus point that lies under the Palace of Thunku.'

'And what's going to happen?' asked Robin anxiously.

'An earthquake. We've got to get out of here!'

The rumbling grew louder. They raced away as fast as their legs could carry them. The walls were beginning to crack and the earth to tremble.

'Quick, quick! Faster!' urged Quadehar, with Agatha in his arms, her feet still bound with a rope.

'Ahhhh!' screamed Coral, as a marble slab crashed down from the ceiling, narrowly missing her.

A guard, who had been hot on their heels, cried out, his legs crushed by a monumental column which had thundered down on top of him.

Robin staggered and lost his balance, landing on the edge of a gaping crack in the floor. Amber, who was keeping as close to Robin as his shadow, grabbed his shoulders and dragged him away from the bottomless abyss.

'Thank you!'

'Later. Hurry!'

Meanwhile, Romaric was having a tough time with a flagging Coral, who had to be dragged along, and Godfrey, who had to be coaxed to keep going amid the rubble and collapsing walls. An Ork fell howling into a gaping chasm a few steps away from them.

'This way!' yelled Quadehar in the lead.

The building was collapsing with a terrifying din, as if the earth itself were being torn open.

'I did this. It was me!' said Robin over and over again, swearing that if he got out of this alive, he would never use the Graphems again in this truly uncertain world.

'Keep going,' Quadehar encouraged them, 'we're

nearly there!'

In front of them, the sunlight streamed in through a gaping hole in the wall and they ran even faster.

They had just distanced themselves from the palace when it collapsed completely, before the astonished eyes of the guards and the dismal population of Yadigar thronging through the streets. The friends slipped discreetly between two older buildings.

'Follow me,' commanded the sorcerer. 'As soon as they come to their senses, we'll have the whole city looking for us.'

Quadehar led them through a maze of narrow streets. Passing Agatha over to Godfrey and Romaric, he marched ahead of the little group.

He strode quickly, and the others sometimes had to run to keep up with him.

Robin, who was just behind Quadehar, waited for his master to scold him.

'Robin!' exploded the sorcerer, 'Robin! Have you any idea what you've done? Using a pigeon and the seal of the Guild for personal messages. Leaving Gifdu in that manner, like a thief. Then opening The Door to The Uncertain World and dragging your friends along with you!'

Robin was ashen. But Quadehar soon calmed down and there was even a smile hovering on his lips. 'If Thomas hadn't described the spell you used to open The Door so accurately, I think I'd have taken him for a madman. Our Chief Sorcerer stood there openmouthed!'

Robin sensed that the scolding was over.

'Master, I had to do it. I don't know why, but I had to.'

Quadehar wasn't listening. He was frowning, as though something was bothering him. 'What surprises me, Robin, is that the spell worked properly, even though you forgot to include Wunjo in your Galdr.'

Robin cleared his throat.

'Er, actually, Master, since you mention it ...'

'We'll talk about it later, my boy,' broke in the sorcerer, 'for the time being, all that matters is that you're all safe and sound.'

Quadehar stopped in front of a low door. He took a big bunch of keys out of his bag, selected one and slid it into the lock.

'We Pursuers need hideaways all over the place,' explained the sorcerer to the dumbfounded friends. 'The door to this world is so far away on the Islands, that we need some more convenient refuges.'

They entered a windowless room. Quadehar locked the door behind them and lit an oil lamp. 'We'll be safe here for a while.'

'How long?' asked Robin.

'It all depends how keen Thunku is to track us down,' replied Quadehar in a weary voice. 'And I'm afraid he's prepared to move heaven and earth to find you.'

'But why?' groaned the apprentice.

'Someone wants you, my boy, and is prepared to pay the price. ... I've told you before, you have extraordinary magic powers! And special powers arouse envy. Including that of a creature like The Shadow, who was unquestionably behind your capture.'

Robin did not reply. Even though he knew, after hearing it from the mouth of the Chief Sorcerer himself, at Gifdu, that The Shadow was after him, he still wasn't convinced. But his master wasn't going to say any more on the subject, that was certain. He kept these thoughts to himself and turned to his companions, who were as relieved as he was to be in one piece and to have found a place of safety. Meanwhile, Quadehar, looking tired and strained, was deep in thought.

'Wow, Robin, when you get mad, do you get mad!' said Romaric, clapping his cousin on the shoulder.

'You know what?' added Godfrey. 'When you're like that, you remind me of Sauron himself!'

'Is that supposed to be a compliment?' queried Robin.

'Coming from a musician, I'm not so sure!' said Romaric.

The three of them kept up their banter to cheer themselves up.

Agatha, in the meantime, was letting out her pent-up misery by crying on Coral's shoulder. Even Amber forgot her dislike of the girl and said a few comforting words. Then, when Agatha had fallen into an exhausted sleep, the friends gathered around Quadehar.

39

Illumination

'It's incredible! So there are several Doors to The Uncertain World?'

'Yes, Master,' confirmed Robin. 'In any case, at least five: there's the official one on the Middle Islands, that you came through. Then there's the one in the Moving Hills, where Amber and I ended up, the one on the People of the Sea's raft, where Coral landed, the one on the beach near Yenibohor where Romaric found himself, and, lastly, the one in the tower of Jaghatel that Godfrey escaped from. Although I'm not sure that they are always visible.'

'Very interesting,' mused the sorcerer. Then he turned to Godfrey: 'Now you say that one room in this tower was full of books and strange instruments?'

'Yes, Master Quadehar,' said the young musician.

'Very interesting,' repeated Quadehar. 'Is there anything else?'

'My headaches!' said Amber, returning to the attack.

Her friends laughed.

'Be quiet, all of you!' ordered Quadehar, then continued in a reassuring tone, 'it is an unusual occurrence, Amber, but there's a perfectly straightforward explanation. The effects of the magic on different people depend on their nature. It's possible that you're more sensitive than the others.'

'Master Quadehar,' asked Godfrey looking deadly serious, 'you say nature, but you mean brain size, don't you? Ow! Ow!'

Once again it took all the sorcerer's authority to restore calm and rescue Godfrey from Amber's clutches. At the same time, a commotion in the street put them on their guard. Thunku's men were searching the town.

'There's no point in our staying here,' announced Quadehar. 'Sooner or later they'll find us. Our only chance now is to try and leave, and get to one of the doors through which you arrived. The one in the Moving Hills appears to be the closest. It's very risky, but we have no choice.'

Robin hesitated for a moment, then took a step towards his master. 'Yes we do. There is, perhaps, another possibility. The Men of the Sands hold this strange ceremony,' he explained. 'During the ceremony, they all hold hands and weave in and out like a snake ...'

'All together?' interrupted Coral.

'Yes, all in a line behind their chief. They call it the Ceremony of the Dead Moon. Do you know why?' said Robin.

'Of course not,' replied Romaric with a shrug. 'How

would we know that?'

'Well,' went on Robin. 'Because they hold it on moonless nights.'

'So?' asked Coral.

'What is especially bright, on moonless nights?'

'The stars, of course,' said Quadehar who was beginning to see what Robin was driving at.

'What surprised me, in this ceremony,' Robin went on excitedly, 'is how similar it is to the magic opening of The Doors: everybody holds hands, and adopts different Stadha – the postures of the Graphems; and the chief even recites a sort of Galdr!'

'What are you on about?' asked Romaric.

'Be quiet,' warned Quadehar. Turning back to Robin, 'Go on, please.'

'So, I connected all that to the legend that says that once upon a time the Men of the Sands used to pass from one world to the next as they pleased ...'

'Which could mean,' broke in Quadehar with a delighted smile, 'that the Men of the Sands possess a very ancient spell that enables people to travel between the worlds without using a Door. That is marvellous! We must go at once to the Ravenous Desert and ...'

'There's no need, Master,' interrupted Robin. 'I wrote down all we need to know about the ceremony in my notebook.'

The sorcerer gave him a great hug, almost suffocating him. 'Well done, Robin. I'm so proud of you.'

Then, surrounded by the others, who silently tried to follow what was going on, master and pupil immersed themselves in the black leather-bound notebook.

'In my opinion, they seem to be carrying out the ritual correctly. If something's going wrong, it's not there.'

'You are right, my boy. But, look – can't you see anything odd in the Stadha?'

Robin looked at the drawings that faithfully reproduced the Graphems he already knew. 'No, I ...'

He stopped in mid-sentence. It was as clear as daylight. 'I get it! The Graphems they invoke for their ceremony are those of The Lost Isle! In The Uncertain World, they are different shapes, because the constellations are slightly distorted in a different sky! That's why the Graphems I called up when I was in the market at Ferghana and in Thunku's palace looked so odd, and neither Isaz nor Thursaz reacted as I expected! The ritual that the Men of the Sands perform in the desert must be the one they saw for the last time, before they crossed from The Lost Isle to The Uncertain World! To go back the other way, they should have changed their ritual according to the different positions of the stars, and therefore the new shapes of the Graphems!'

Robin leaped up and punched the air in delight. Mystified, his friends stared blankly at him, while the sorcerer gazed fondly at his pupil.

Then they both sat down and transcribed the spell according to the parameters of the sky and stars in The Uncertain World.

While all this was going on, to pass the time, Amber and Coral competed against Godfrey and Romaric in a game from The Lost Isle which involved looking at a set of objects for one minute then seeing who could remember the most when they looked away. It kept them all amused and distracted from the danger all around them.

The girls won both rounds hands down, as always and, as always, the boys accused them of cheating. At last, the sorcerer and his apprentice looked up.

'That's it,' announced Quadehar triumphantly. 'We're ready!'

Just then, there was a violent banging at the door.

'Hurry up, we don't have a second to lose!'

Coral quickly woke Agatha who was still fast asleep. Then, on Quadehar's instructions, they all held hands, as they had done originally when they'd gone through the door between the two worlds. Meanwhile something large and hairy was trying to smash the door down with an axe but, thanks to Quadehar's spells, it was holding up, for now.

'Agatha, will you be all right?' inquired Quadehar.

She nodded. She had regained a little strength during those few hours' rest, and felt a lot better.

'Right. Now the process is a bit more complicated than the one Robin used with you on The Lost Isle,' explained Quadehar. 'We don't have a door, and we're going to have to create one! To do that, each one of us in turn, without letting go of the others' hands, must imitate with our body the shapes of the Graphems for the crossing into the other world. I'll recite the spell while we do it. ... Pay attention, concentrate and we'll be fine. We only have one chance. Are you ready?'

They nodded apprehensively.

'Are you sure that we won't get split up again and all end up in different places?' Coral couldn't help worrying aloud.

'Don't be concerned,' Romaric reassured her. 'We've got a real sorcerer with us this time!'

Amber, who, to everyone's surprise, had automatically sprung to Robin's defence since they'd been reunited, looked daggers at Romaric. Quadehar implored them all not to waste time. Quickly he went through eight different postures, corresponding to eight Graphems of The Uncertain World. Agatha, Coral, Amber, Godfrey, Romaric and Robin carefully imitated his every move. The sorcerer chanted the Galdr.

After he had uttered the last incantation, they heard, as they had done several days before on The Lost Isle, the creaking sound of a door opening. The room they were in faded. Once again, they were sucked into a terrifying whirlwind and plunged into a dark hole.

*

'There was what? An earthquake ... that's no excuse ... Lomgo. ...'

In the grey stone-walled chamber crammed with books and evil-looking instruments, the scribe waited for the storm to blow over. Before his eyes, his master, shrouded by the shadows that followed him everywhere, exploded in a fit of rage. 'You had him ... and you let him go. ... Why?'

'Because of the sorcerer, Master. He came and rescued the child. Even Thunku was powerless to stop him.'

The menacing figure let out a howl of fury, then

became still. 'Let's see. I need to think.'

The master was talking to himself. Although he was accustomed to his outbursts, Lomgo was relieved that calm was restored.

'He will be mine, by hook or by crook. He must be ...'

In the half-dark, the shadowy figure continued talking to himself, filling the room with his loud mutterings.

'I must find a way. ...'

Seeing that the master had no further need for him, Lomgo discreetly withdrew.

'The boy ... the boy must be mine ... mine.'

40

Back on The Lost Isle

They emerged together right in the middle of a beautiful heath that was familiar to them all. In the distance, they glimpsed the sparkling ocean.

'Korrigans heath! Korrigans heath!' exclaimed Romaric. 'We're back home! We did it!'

They shouted for joy and began to run in all directions. Coral even kissed Quadehar on the cheek.

'Whoa, whoa!' said the sorcerer who was feeling more emotional than he wanted to show. 'Don't let's hang around, it's getting dark. 'The Korrigans are probably watching and already cooking up some tricks to play on us.'

So they all set off for Dashtikazar, laughing and chatting as people do when they survive an adventure that could so easily have ended badly.

'Master Quadehar, you haven't told us how you knew we'd been taken prisoner by Thunku,' Godfrey said, walking alongside him with Romaric and Coral.

'Do you know a giant covered in scars who answers to the name of Tofann?' the sorcerer asked. 'Well, after emerging through The Door, I headed straight for Ferghana, the nearest town, thinking that you'd probably had the same idea. In Ferghana, I learned that a Little Man had helped a young slave to escape. Knowing that some grey cloaks had gone missing from Gifdu, and that it wasn't customary for the people of Virdu to help their neighbours, I immediately thought of you! My search then took me to the Ravenous Desert, and then the Stone Road, where I met Tofann who put me on your trail. There. No wizard cunning involved!'

'Master Quadehar,' asked Godfrey again, 'why did Thunku call you Azhdar the Demon?'

'I frequently upset his plans, so I am a demon as far as Thunku's concerned! Besides, I should have realized straight away that he was somehow mixed up in this kidnapping business. As for Azhdar, that's the name I use when I'm in The Uncertain World. Any more questions?'

Romaric turned to Quadehar.

'Yes, Master Sorcerer. Why are so many people interested in Robin – the Guild, The Shadow, and you?'

'I can't answer you my boy, because I don't know yet. Or rather, I can only repeat the same answer, and that is because he has profound magical powers.'

'And that makes people envious, I know. But how can you explain the fact that after just three months, Robin is able to do things that take other sorcerers long years of hard work?' said Romaric

'Hard work isn't everything, Romaric. In all

professions there are people who are more gifted than others. ...'

Romaric wasn't satisfied with this answer, but, like his cousin, he kept his disappointment to himself, promising he'd do his utmost to find out the secret behind Robin's special skills.

Quadehar changed the subject. 'Do you realize, children, that you're going to be real heroes on The Lost Isle?'

'Heroes? How come?' asked Coral.

'Think about it. You've journeyed to The Uncertain World, and you've come back to tell the tale, even though you aren't Pursuers. That's unheard of! What's more, you haven't come back empty-handed, you've returned Agatha Balangru to her father, having snatched her from the clutches of a fearful tyrant. And, you've brought a valuable spell that had been lost for centuries back to the Guild! What else does it take to become a hero?'

All this time, bringing up the rear, Robin had been thinking. It was still too soon for it all to sink in. The events of the last week had happened so quickly. In their adventure in The Uncertain World and in Master Quadehar's explanations, there was something that didn't quite add up, and it was bothering him. He felt vaguely that they were all on the wrong track, that there was more to the story, even though he couldn't say exactly what. It was all still a muddle in his mind.

He was soon joined by Amber and Agatha. The atmosphere immediately became strained. Amber couldn't bear the way Agatha now looked at her friend Robin.

'Robin,' Agatha suddenly asked, 'did you and your friends really take all those risks to come and free me?'

'Er ... yes,' he replied, wondering what she was driving at.

'Despite everything I did to you at school, you came to my rescue?' went on Agatha.

'There's a difference between losing a pendant and being condemned to sweep floors for the rest of your life with your legs in chains!' Robin laughed.

Agatha stopped dead in the middle of the path. 'Robin, I have something important to tell you.'

'Steady, girl,' Amber objected, moving towards Agatha, her fists bunching.

'Calm down, Amber, calm down,' said Robin. 'Agatha, you can speak in front of Amber, I have no secrets from my friends.'

'No. What I have to tell you is for your ears only.'

Amber darted a look at Robin that was both threatening and pleading. He sighed. Amber's behaviour since they had met up again had been baffling.

After a moment, he said, 'Amber, would you go and join the others for a moment. Please.'

Amber flashed a look of resentment at Agatha, then walked away grumbling.

Robin turned to Agatha. 'Now, what do you have to say to me that is so important?'

'At first, I was planning to keep this to myself ... but then I realized that you have a right to know. Even if it's only a very vague piece of information and nothing to get excited about.'

'Go on, then,' Robin sighed again, 'I'm listening.'

'Well, here goes. One evening I overheard a conversation between Thunku and his Councillor. That ex-priest is worse than his master, believe me! Anyway, they were talking in hushed tones about Lord Sha.'

'Sha? I've already heard that name somewhere. ...'

'Lord Sha lives in a tower, beside the Vast Ocean. Not much is known about him. He's said to have awesome powers. He isn't exactly liked, but that doesn't mean he's all bad, either. Actually, people are just afraid of him. I think Thunku is his only friend. If you can call that monster a friend!'

'Come on, spit it out,' said Robin, growing impatient.

'They were wondering if Sha would ever find the son who was stolen from him at birth, and who he's never seen. A son who would be about twelve now. Now as I know that someone is desperately trying to kidnap you, and as Lord Sha is in league with Thunku, I wondered ...'

She didn't finish her sentence. Robin was looking straight into Agatha's eyes. He was absolutely calm, but his heart was thumping madly.

'Thank you, Agatha,' he finally said, in a slightly unsteady voice. 'Even if I'm not sure yet what I can do about this revelation.'

They remained still and silent for a moment.

In the end, Agatha spoke shyly, 'I think they're waiting for us.'

Robin felt himself emerge as if from a dream. A little further on, sitting on a boulder, Amber was watching them, her arms folded.

'You're right. Let's go.'

Walking along the path, Robin added, 'You swear you won't say a word to anybody?'

'I promise.'

They joined Amber, then all three of them ran to catch up with their friends.

It was that hour when the setting sun is nothing but a faint glow and the first stars are beginning to twinkle in the night sky.

END OF PART 1

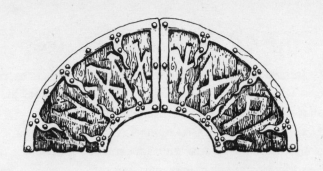

ROBIN'S NOTEBOOK

THE GRAPHEM ALPHABET

The Graphems are the 24 letters of a magic alphabet, based on the stars, which make it possible to enter the Wyrd. They are like keys that unlock and reveal the secrets inside.

A Graphem is defined by its number (order and position within the group), its shape (name and appearance), its content (symbolic associations, other names and powers).

Each Graphem has several powers. When Graphems are mentally summoned (visualised) then projected (shouted or whispered), they have a simple and direct effect.

> **Example:** to open a locked door, I concentrate and think
> very hard about the Graphem Elhaz (it appears in my mind)
> and I whisper or shout its name (depending on how stiff
> the door is).

THE WYRD

The Wyrd is like a giant spider's web whose threads are attached to everything that exists. The Graphems are the key to entering the Wyrd, making it possible to act on all these connections. Understanding and controlling the Wyrd and its mechanisms is the secret of magic.

But be careful: since everything is connected to everything else within the Wyrd, a tiny act can have enormous consequences. That is why prudence and humility are the sorcerer's motto!

And that is why you have to work very hard and gain a lot of experience to become knowledgeable. Master Quadehar keeps telling me: 'From act to act, the act will guide you. From word to word, the word will guide you.'

THE GALDR

This is a spell using combinations of Graphems. The Galdr links different powers. Graphems are like words, a Galdr is like a sentence. But the names of the Graphems alone are not enough.

When a sorcerer uses a Graphem on its own, he creates a relationship between dominant (the sorcerer making the spell) and dominated (the Graphem invoked). The Graphem automatically responds to its name.

But in a Galdr, the sorcerer links two equal Graphems together. To do this, he has to tame them and make them work together by evoking their other names.

Example: The Galdr for going through the door to the Uncertain World. This is a fairly simple one as it only uses two Graphems (actually, the spell that is carved into the door is much more complicated and very powerful and that's what opens the door. My Galdr simply sets it in motion). I call Raidhu, the travel Graphem, and Eiwaz, which allows communication between the two worlds. In my mind, I force them to approach and accept each other. That sometimes takes a long time!

Then I ask them to cooperate: *'By the power of the Way, of Nerthus, (Raidhu's other name) Ullr and of the Double Branch (Eiwaz's other name), Raidhu (the chariot) below and Eiwaz (the opener) in front, take me! RE!'*

THE OND

While the Wyrd is the source of magic and the Graphems are the instruments of sorcery, it is the Ond that makes magic practice possible.

The Ond is the sorcerer's inner force, which charges the Graphems with energy. That is why some sorcerers are more powerful than others: some have a strong Ond, others a weak one. There's nothing you can do about it, it's the way you are born. But, as Master Quadehar is always reminding me, having a strong Ond doesn't excuse you from having to study and train hard!

THE STADHA

The power of the Graphems can be reinforced with postures imitating their shape: these are the Stadha. By reproducing the shape of the Graphems, you charge up your Ond (inner force) by capturing external energies (such as ley lines, for example). A Graphem combined with a Stadha has much more power and impact.

All these secrets to do with magic, beginning with the revelation about the Graphems, come from a very ancient book called the **Book of the Stars**. It contains lots of other secrets that the sorcerers haven't deciphered yet. It was stolen many years ago and nobody knows where it is now.

THE CONSTELLATIONS

In the Uncertain World, the positions of the stars in the sky are different from those of the Lost Isle. That's why the Graphems, which are based on certain constellations, do not have exactly the same form as in the Lost Isle.

But they do retain the same powers, with a few variations.

To use them, you have to adapt them (find the corresponding form in the sky of The Uncertain World) and reappropriate them in their new form.

CORVUS (THE CROW) ∏ Wuz

GEMINI (THE TWINS) ᚲ Perthro

LUPUS (THE WOLF) ᛞ Dagaz

PLEIADES ᚠ Fehu

THE GRAPHEM ALPHABET

So far my master has taught me the following 12 letters:

FEHU (f)

Position: first Graphem
Other names: Spider web
Associations: creation (cosmic fire) – wealth (cattle)
Powers: changes objects into energy, captures cosmic energy
Stadha (position): stand sideways and raise both arms just above shoulder level, the right arm slightly higher than the left

URUZ (u/v)

Position: second Graphem
Other names: Russet cow
Associations: ancient archaic powers (rain) – the source (Grandmother)
Powers: pacifies the spirits of a place – roots and structures enhances the effect of plants – captures earthly energy
Stadha (position): bend from the waist and touch the ground with your hands

THURSAZ (t)

Position: third Graphem
Other names: The Antelope head, The Mountain
Associations: attack, defence, (thorn)
Powers: protects (if projected) and captures underground energy
Stadha (position): stand straight with your left hand on your hip

DANGEROUS GRAPHEM!

BE CAREFUL!

USE WITH CAUTION

RAIDHU (r)

Position: fifth Graphem
Other names: Reginn, Nerthus, The Way
Associations: travel (chariot)
Powers: transports, gives coherence, organises and arranges, governs correspondences, concentrates strength (spiral energy) – essential for transformations
Stadha (position): stand on your right leg, put your left hand on your hip and extend your left leg, resting the heel on the ground, the toe pointing upwards

WUNJO (w)

Position: eighth Graphem
Other names: The Generous, The Standard
Associations: joy and harmony – gathering the members of a clan
Powers: protects groups – harmonises the actions of the different Graphems and helps them work together
Stadha (position): stand straight with your right hand by your side, and touch the left side of your head with your left hand, bending it at the elbow

NAUDHIZ (n)

Position: tenth Graphem
Other names: The Hand
Associations: necessity and distress (the fire of survival) – obligations linked to destiny (awareness)
Powers: neutralises magic spells – resists attack – awakens (the self)
Stadha (position): stand with your feet together, raise your right hand up in the air at a 45% angle and make a diagonal with your left hand at 45% from your side

ISAZ (i)

Position: eleventh Graphem
Other names: The Brilliant
Associations: primal immobility (ice) – self control (anti-movement)
Powers: draws in energy to the self, condenses, retains – aids concentrations and reinforces the will
Stadha (position): stand straight with your arms by your sides

EIWAZ (e)

Position: thirteenth Graphem (central)

DANGEROUS GRAPHEM!

Other names: Ullr, The Double Branch
Associations: the axe, (the yew tree)
Powers: enables communication between the worlds (the opener)
Stadha (position): turn sideways, stand on your left foot, put your right foot out behind you, resting on the toes, hands held out a few inches either side at hip level

BE CAREFUL!
USE WITH CAUTION

PERTHRO (p)

Position: fourteenth Graphem

DANGEROUS GRAPHEM!

Other names: The Auspicious, The Matrix
Associations: the guide in the Wyrd (dice cup) and maze-like paths
Powers: associated with destiny and its laws – contains the mystery of the Wyrd – releases, transforms
Stadha (position): sit down, raise your knees and draw your feet towards you, rest your elbows on your knees

BE CAREFUL!
USE WITH CAUTION

ELHAZ (z)

Position: fifteenth Graphem
Other names: Njord, The Ancestor
Associations: life, the soul (the swan)
Powers: removes locks, thaws difficult situations (crackles when it burns) resists hostile forces – magic protection
Stadha (position): stand with feet together and both arms outstretched

INGWAZ (ng/gn)

Position: twenty-second Graphem
Other names: Ing, The Wealthy
Associations: masculine energy, freezing
Powers: concentration of energies – talisman – immobilisation (nail)
Stadha (position): stand with feet together and bend your arms to form a triangle with your hands on top of your head

DAGAZ (d)

Position: twenty-third Graphem
Other names: The Day, The Knights
Associations: soft daylight – the eternal return (each time different) – the mystery of time lapses
Powers: fights evil spirits, protects from harmful events – makes you invisible – shapes and suspends time
Stadha (position): stand straight with your arms crossed over your chest